Loosely Engaged

By the same author

A Different World: Stories of Great Hotels
Diary of a Somebody
The Long-Haired Boy

Loosely Engaged

Further pages from the Diary of a Somebody

CHRISTOPHER MATTHEW
Illustrations by Phillida Gili

Hutchinson
London Melbourne Sydney Auckland Johannesburg

Hutchinson & Co. (Publishers) Ltd

An imprint of the Hutchinson Publishing Group

3 Fitzroy Square, London W1P 6JD

Hutchinson Group (Australia) Pty Ltd
30–32 Cremorne Street, Richmond South, Victoria 3121
PO Box 151, Broadway, New South Wales 2007

Hutchinson Group (NZ) Ltd
32–34 View Road, PO Box 40–086, Glenfield, Auckland 10

Hutchinson Group (SA) (Pty) Ltd
PO Box 337, Bergvlei 2012, South Africa

First published 1980
© Christopher Matthew 1980
Illustrations © Hutchinson Publishing Group 1980

Set in Monotype Garamond

Printed in Great Britain by The Anchor Press Ltd
and bound by Wm Brendon & Son Ltd
both of Tiptree, Essex

ISBN 0 09 142830 0

To Nicholas, with love

To Nicholas, with love

Sunday, June 11th

Villa Les Roches Blanches, Cap d'Antibes.

What an extraordinary thing life can be at times. One minute,
all is sweetness and light. The sky above is blue and the way
ahead seems straight and untrammelled. The next, dark
storm clouds have gathered overhead and suddenly the road
is strewn with sharp stones and pot-holes at every turn.

It is a mere week since I closed my diary for the last time,
confident that, with my new-found love for Amanda Trubshawe and my promotion to Assistant Group Head, I should
have neither the time nor the need for introspection. Yet
already I feel the urge to take up my pen once more and
commit my innermost thoughts to paper. I am only sorry I
did not bring my faithful old diary down with me. However,
the cheap exercise book I bought in Antibes will have
to serve for another week. Is there really still a week to go?
Frankly, there have been days when I have felt like buying
my own ticket and taking the next plane to London. However, when one is the guest of one's chairman and his wife –
not to say the boyfriend of their daughter – it is not only bad
manners to walk out, but very bad public relations. It is also
extremely expensive. I see no alternative but to stay and see
the holiday out. Unfortunately, no amount of hot sunshine,
beautiful surroundings, excellent food and wines, and
twice-daily water-skiing can disguise the fact that relations
between Amanda and me have turned decidedly frosty.
I am sorry that I do not share her enthusiasm for the Pot à
Gogo discotheque or for lounging around in cafés, with dark-

7

skinned layabouts, smoking Gitanes and talking twaddle, but there it is.

As I said to her, I somehow can't imagine the Scott Fitzgeralds and the Gerald Murphys frittering their time away on the Riviera on such mindless pastimes, but the names mean nothing to her. I suppose this is one of the penalties one has to pay for falling in love with a girl half one's age.

Matters not made any easier by my feelings toward Enid Trubshawe which are equivocal, to say the least. I continue to find her tremendously attractive and I'm pretty sure she feels the same way about me.

On reflection, it was perhaps unwise of me to have agreed to travel down alone with her in the Rolls. Even though nothing actually happened at the hotel in Orange, it could have, which amounts to the same thing.

How very confusing it all is.

The sun doesn't seem to be doing my rash much good either.

Monday, June 12th

The chairman has had to fly back to London on unexpected business. Strongly tempted to ask if I could join him. However, Enid suggested that after dropping him at Nice Airport we should drive up to Saint Paul-de-Vence for lunch at the Colombe d'Or. The opportunity to experience one of the great restaurants of the world is not one that should be lightly dismissed. Luckily we had a table outside on the terrace. Amanda silently intent on her sun-tan, as usual, until Enid mentioned that the last time she had been there she had seen Dirk Bogarde having a drink in the bar. At this A. perked up no end, leaving the table at frequent intervals and disappearing indoors.

When I asked her if he was there, she said. 'Who?'

I said, 'Dirk Bogarde, of course.'

She said, 'I've no idea. I was looking for Jean-Jacques. He said he might be here.'

I asked her who Jean-Jacques was. 'Oh', she said, 'just someone I met at the discothèque.'

Her mother said nothing and neither did I. But honestly. . . .

Think I may have spotted Graham Greene in the street this evening. It's reassuring to know that the literary tradition of the Riviera is alive and well. Am rather hoping I might have the chance to meet him sometime. Although of different generations, we have remarkably similar minds.

Tuesday, June 13th

Swam, sun-bathed and wind-surfed the whole day. I really believe I'm getting the hang of this curious sport at last. Managed to stand for several minutes on end without toppling into the water. Haven't quite mastered turning yet, or indeed moving forward, but it's only a matter of time. I daresay I do look a little ungainly compared with the skinny local boys whom Amanda seems to attract in such numbers; but then, of course, it's easy enough to acquire a flashy superficial skill in these fringe sports if you have nothing else to do all day, and I feel Amanda's unstinted admiration for their self-conscious cavortings is disproportionately enthusiastic.

When I made a pointed comment to this effect, Amanda said, 'I'm not making any comparisons. We all of us have our different talents.'

We certainly do. I'd like to see some of those sun-tanned merchants trying to compile a Barford New Product Development proposal document.

In the evening played Scrabble and won every game! It's a relief to know I'm good at something.

Drank three cognacs and went to bed feeling decidedly more cheerful than for several days.

Pity I had to catch the sun again quite so badly across my shoulders. I thought I'd surmounted that hurdle last week.

Wednesday, June 14th

After breakfast Enid drove to Nice to collect Derrick from London.

Sun-bathed with Amanda in the garden.

Object of the exercise almost totally nullified in my case owing to having to wear an aertex shirt and a towel across the top of my legs to protect nasty sunburn. Amanda even darker brown than usual in the briefest bikini I have ever seen. I seem to remember reading somewhere that some

9

people have more oil in their skin than others. I'm not surprised; she certainly puts enough of the stuff on. After a while she took off her bikini top. I said, 'Are you sure that's wise?'

'Very,' she said. 'Why?'

I said, 'We wouldn't want your parents to arrive back suddenly and get the wrong idea.'

She said, 'What sort of wrong ideas could they possibly get? We're going together, aren't we? Supposed to be, anyway.'

I said that the fact that one was going out with a girl did not automatically entitle one to play the goat in broad daylight at eleven o'clock in the morning.

She replied that I didn't seem to be interested in playing the goat at any time of the day or night.

Oh dear. I was afraid that this touchy subject would raise its ugly head sooner or later. The truth is, I shall be quite ready to play my full part in this regard as and when the time is right. Our love is still in its blossoming stage and I feel that, if we wish it to ripen and produce an abundance of fruit, to pluck the flowers at this early stage would be rash and foolish.

Also, the problem of hanky-panky in other people's houses is always a tricky one – viz: the humiliating incident at Jane's parents' in Oxted. Funnily enough, I have dreamt about Jane once or twice recently. I cannot imagine why.

By way of a welcome-home for the chairman, Enid cooked an absolutely delicious *pintade à la Rousillonne* which Derrick complemented, as usual, with some first-class burgundy. What a joy it is to be marrying into a family of real gourmets. It's all a very far cry from the middle-class fare dished up by Jane's parents.

Sorry to discover later as I was undressing that, despite my careful precautions this afternoon, my skin is even redder and more painful than before. I can scarcely lie down without experiencing severe discomfort. This will definitely put any 'goat-playing' out of court for several days.

Thursday, June 15th

To the Grand Hotel du Cap for lunch at the Eden Roc pavilion. One has the feeling that at any second one will look up and glimpse Scott and Zelda, the Murphys, Ernest and

Pablo strolling through the pines in their bathing wraps, sipping dry martinis and swapping amusing repartee. Amanda certainly in sparkling form.

Lunched extremely well off cold *loup de mer* and Pouilly Fumé at one of the umbrella-ed tables on the terrace overlooking the pool. While waiting for coffee, thought I'd take a few snaps of the lunchtime scene purely for reference purposes, so moved amongst the tables with my Instamatic, snapping away at random rather as I imagine Tony Snowdon does when he's working on an assignment. My discreet and casual manner obviously paid off, since most people took no notice of me at all. Was quite surprised, therefore, when one stout, rather red-faced couple waved their arms at me as I passed their table and said, in English, 'Not for us, thanks.' I stopped and asked them what they meant. 'Oh,' said the man in an unmistakably North Country accent, 'aren't you one of them beach photographers then?'

I replied that I was certainly no such thing.

His wife said, 'You look just like one in your dungarees.'

I said nothing and returned to my table. How people who cannot tell the difference between 'dungarees' and a pair of extremely well-cut jeans manage to get past the doorman of a place like the Eden Roc, let alone afford the prices, I simply cannot comprehend. They must feel so terribly out of place. And yet, only moments afterwards, I saw the head waiter dancing attendance on them. As I remarked this evening to Enid, 'Scott and Zelda must be turning in their graves.'

She said, 'He might, she wouldn't. She was burned to death in a fire.'

What a pleasure it is to be in the company of such a witty, well-read woman.

Friday, June 16th

Life with the Trubshawes is a non-stop round of pleasure. This evening we drove to Monte Carlo for dinner at the Hotel de Paris. An excellent and, as it has turned out, unique opportunity to wear Tim Pedalow's white dinner jacket.

A pity my nose had to choose today of all days to start peeling. Even so, everyone commented on the jacket, and in the car Amanda squeezed my arm, gave me a kiss and said, 'Ooh, I quite fancy you this evening.' I whispered back, 'Me too,' at which Enid called out from the front seat, 'Come along now, you two love-birds.' I felt rather foolish.

Dinner in the huge, ornate dining room excellent. On a platform at the far end, a small orchestra played suitably old-fashioned melodies. At one point the violinist strolled round the tables asking for requests. I asked for 'The Man Who Broke the Bank at Monte Carlo'. He gave me a blank look, announced that he had never heard of it and moved on to the next table. Some sort of joke, I imagine.

Amanda spent much of the meal singing the praises of Bjorn Borg, the tennis player who, I gather, lives in Monte Carlo, though goodness knows why.

After dinner, Derrick announced that he fancied trying his hand at the tables. This was excellent news. I have always wanted to see the famous casino, and a visit to Monte without chancing a bob or two on the green baize would be as unthinkable as driving through Avignon without stopping to look at the *pont*.

Suggested they go on ahead while I took a short walk to settle a slight attack of indigestion. After a while, felt slightly better and made my way into the sumptuously decorated interior of the most famous gaming rooms in the world. Surprised to fine most of the players dressed in a most casual way. Some were even wearing jeans. No sign of the Trubshawes. Made enquiries of one of the employees. He looked me up and down and said, 'I think your friends must be at the new Sporting Club down on the beach.'

Took a taxi, which cost me all the money I would otherwise have splurged on the tables. Just as well, probably, since all the Trubshawes lost theirs. But then, of course, they can afford to. I have better things to do with my money than chuck it away in such joyless and fruitless pastimes. The philosophy of something for nothing is thoroughly alien to me, and for all his great writing, it certainly brought little happiness to Dostoievsky.

Was strolling around, hand in hand with Amanda, when an American couple came up and asked her if she was Princess Caroline. I don't know if they thought I was Philippe Junot. I hope not.

Saturday, June 17th

Our last day at Les Roches Blanches. Am really quite sorry to be going, even though, from a romantic point of view, the holiday has been very much of a curate's egg.

But then, in my experience, everyone's judgement tends to go to pieces when they're abroad, and I am confident that we shall quickly find ourselves on the same wave-length once we are back in London.

For all her childish ways and unformed tastes, Amanda still sets my heart skipping every time I see her, and I am certain that beneath that frivolous exterior her feelings for me are as genuine and serious as ever. Really, my head is in as much of a whirl as it was before the holiday began. We leave tomorrow after lunch. Enid and Amanda and I take the plane; the chairman drives home in the Rolls. No mention of my accompanying *him*, I'm glad to say.

Sunday, June 18th

While buying croissants for breakfast in Antibes, bumped into the head waiter from the Eden Roc. I hardly recognized him in mufti. He certainly didn't recognize me, but then in that sort of job one must meet so many people.

Had a most interesting conversation about the hotel. Happened to mention the elderly North Country couple who had seemed so obviously out of place the other day.

'Ah, yes, *monsieur*,' he said, 'Sir Eric and Lady Maxwell. A charming couple. They have been coming to the Grand Hotel ever since they had their honeymoon here in 1928. They were great friends of the Scott Fitzgeralds, you know.'

Waiters are such snobs, one never knows if they are telling the truth.

On our way out to the plane at Nice, felt a hand on my shoulder and turned round to find myself face to face with Bryant-Fenn of all people. I gathered he had been on the Riviera for the best part of a week, writing an article for some in-flight magazine about the Monegasque royal family. He nodded towards Enid and murmured, 'Isn't that the woman I saw you with at the theatre a week or two back?' I told him I really couldn't remember. 'Yes, you do,' he persisted. 'I asked you who she was the next day and you told me she was your aunt up for the day from Haywards Heath or some-where.'

Attempted to brush him aside but he went on, 'You're a sly one. I congratulate you.' Decided to put an end to this charade once and for all by introducing him to the wife of the chairman of Harley Preston.

'What fun,' he said cheerfully. 'Let's all sit together.' I pointed out that we had specially reserved seats at the back.

'Oh,' he said, 'in that case we can't. I'm travelling first class.'

For nothing presumably, as usual.

As we were taking off, Enid said, 'Who was that? A friend?' I laughed and said, 'Hardly.'

Ten minutes later a stewardess arrived with a bottle of champagne and three glasses, compliments of Monsieur Bryant-Fenn.

Of course I said that we could not possibly accept such a gift from a comparative stranger.

Enid said, 'I don't see why,' and asked the stewardess to pour it out for us.

She took a couple of sips and said, 'It's a pity you don't know a few more people like Mr Bryant-Fenn.'

Arrived back at the flat at ten thirty to find that Jane has moved out, lock, stock and barrel, and gone to live with Armitage in his 'house' in Clapham. It is disappointing enough to think that one's ex-girlfriend should have seen fit to ally herself with the man one has recently ousted as Assistant Group Head, but that she should give up a good address in Holland Park in favour of a shabby workman's cottage in a poor street in South London is beyond my understanding.

No sooner stepped through front door than I was con-fronted by a small, dark, Arabic-looking girl, dressed in shocking green, skin-tight trousers and one of *my* best shirts, tied in a knot at the hip, who said in a rude voice, 'I think you have made a mistake. This is Ralph Beddoes's flat.'

I said, 'On the contrary, it is *you* who have made the mistake. This is *my* flat.'

At that moment, Beddoes emerged from the bedroom wearing just a towelling dressing gown (no prizes for guess-ing what *they'd* been up to) and introduced the girl as his fiancée. He must take me for a fool. Her name is Shusha and she comes, like all bad news these days, from Iran.

'Her family is one of the best in Teheran,' he told me, 'but they have fallen on hard times.'

'So hard apparently that they can't even afford their own shirts,' I said. 'I understood you were leaving for Brussels last week, Beddoes.'

'Well,' he said, 'you obviously understood wrong.'

How he has managed to make such a success in the City with manners like that I can't imagine. As for this new job, I dread to think how he is going to cope at the polite dinner tables of EEC high society. Roy Jenkins will make mincemeat of him, and rightly.

Compelled to eat scrambled eggs to the accompaniment of evil-smelling eastern cooking and toneless, oriental, so-called music on the gramophone.

Also had to sleep without sheets or pillowcases owing to Beddoes' failure to collect clean laundry.

What a wretched homecoming and how I long for a quiet life. Possibly a married one.

Monday, June 19th

My first day as Assistant Group Head and one on which I should have set out fresh and eager to face up to my new responsibilities; yet I do not believe I have ever known a more depressing start to any week. Things got off on the wrong foot at breakfast when Beddoes said, 'I suppose you will be resigning your job at the earliest opportunity.'

I told him I had no intention of doing any such thing.

'Oh well,' he said. 'If you have no scruples about nepotism.'

I laughed and said that it was Armitage who was the chairman's nephew, not me.

He said airily, 'Nephew, son-in-law, it all boils down to the same thing in the end.'

I replied that what was good enough for our ex-ambassador in Washington was certainly good enough for me.

'And look at the trouble that caused,' he said, and marched off into the bathroom.

He may have a point or he may not. Time alone will tell. A real friend, of course, would not have raised the subject in the first place.

Arrived at the office to find that not only had no one made the slightest effort to move my things out of my old office, but that my new room (Armitage's old one) was now occupied by a tall, blonde American girl who announced herself as Ruth Macmichael.

She has recently arrived in London after eight years in a large New York advertising agency and is, I gather, to be my junior assistant.

'I believe that if one is in the business of selling, one should get to have as wide a perspective on the market place as possible,' she announced.

I said I quite agreed, and that as soon as we had the office situation sorted out we must sit down and exchange a few ideas.

She replied that, according to the latest psychological research carried out in America, status symbols at work are a hindrance to positive thinking.

'I mean,' she said, 'who cares a damn whether I have a bigger office than you? How's that going to help shift our clients' products off the supermarket shelves?' If she couldn't see how, I certainly was not about to tell her.

I do hope we're not heading for an ugly confrontation. The omens are far from favourable.

Tuesday, June 20th

Still no progress re my new office. Mentioned the matter to Roundtree, as group head. He *says* he'll look into it. There seems to be an awful lot of talk and very little do in this place nowadays. May very well say something to the chairman next time I see him.

Shortly before lunch, went to see Ruth about the Barford sales figures, only to learn from Sarah that she is away all day on private business.

It is not easy being an Assistant Group Head without a group to be Assistant Head of. Talk about too many chiefs and not enough indians. In the flat, of course, it's quite the reverse – if you can call Persians indians.

Wednesday, June 21st

This evening I said to Amanda, 'I suppose you'll be throwing yourself wholeheartedly into the Season from now on.'

She laughed and said, 'Don't be silly. No one does the Season any more.'

I reminded her that when we first met she'd told me she was doing precisely that.

'Oh yes,' she said, 'but it's only a manner of speech. All that Berkeley Dress Show, Ascot, Goodwood stuff is as out-of-date as the Rolling Stones. Occasionally someone throws a thrash, but most of the time we just bomb round to Wedgies or Tramps and have a bit of a giggle.'

In my opinion, there is no more pathetic sight than that of an older man trying to ingratiate himself with a younger girl by pretending to be *au fait* with her world. On the other hand, one does not wish to appear an old fuddy-duddy, so I remarked casually that I had been quite a dancer myself in my time and had once won a Twist competition during a skiing holiday in the Austrian Tyrol.

Amanda said, 'Oh yes, I've heard of the Twist. I think my parents used to do it.'

Thursday, June 22nd

An astounding thing happened. Strolled into Ruth's office to ask if she would mind collating the Barford projections for tomorrow's meeting.

'Why?' she said, 'Can't you?'

I replied in a light-hearted way that I was her superior and, as such, expected a bit more respect.

'I don't see why,' she said. 'Frankly, as far as I'm concerned, you're a bit of an ass-hole.'

I made it quite clear that I was not about to put up with that sort of talk from anyone by turning and leaving the room without a word.

These Americans are getting above themselves. They are guests in our country, and Harvard Business School or no Harvard Business School, a modicum of politeness and modesty is surely not too much to expect.

Any more of this behaviour and she'll be feeling the rough side of my tongue.

Friday, June 23rd

I thought I had made it perfectly clear, following the unfortunate incident during my visit to the school in May, that I wished to resign from the OF Society and to have no further communication with them. And yet today through the post comes a booklet containing minutes of the annual general meeting of the Society, details of the Society's accounts, reports of the progress of OF Cricket, Rugger, Golf, Fencing, Cross-Country Running, Hockey and Darts, and news of the trivial activities of fifty or more OFs, none of whom I have ever heard of – even though some claim to have been contemporaries.

Of what possible interest can it be to anyone that L. G. Rasper (Brough's, 1949–54) has given up his job as Deputy Agricultural Supervisor in southern Botswana to become Banqueting Manager of the Ibn Bin Saud Palace Motel in Qatar? Or that Andrew Smellie (Newby's, 1970–75) has passed his chartered accountancy exams and has been making a name for himself in the Plymouth area with his mobile discotheque and lighting-à-gogo roadshow? As for the information that Wilfred Ng (Boshier's, 1955–59) 'who will be remembered by all of us for his epic battle against Kenneth Singh (Parkinson's, 1954–58) in the finals of the Pemberton Squash Cup in 1958' (not by me, for one) married the sister of G. G. Cartwright (Lomas's, 1951–56) and now has a son and daughter, it seems to me sheer conceit on the part of Ng to suppose that his private life is of concern to any but his family and most intimate circle of friends. I notice someone has enclosed a roneo-ed sheet of paper with the words, 'I should like the following news of myself published in the OF News section of the school magazine. Name . . . House . . . Dates . . . Address and phone number. . . .'

Strongly tempted to commit it to the waste-paper basket, but have decided on second thoughts to put it away in a safe place until I feel I have something really worthwhile to publish. I only wish more OFs would follow my example.

Saturday, June 24th

Standards are dropping daily. Called in at my local off-licence this evening on way home from the office to buy a bottle of Robinson's Barley Water.

'Sorry, dear,' said the woman behind the counter, 'we've had a bit of a run on cordials.'

I said that I thought she must have misunderstood me; it was not some fizzy peppermint or blackcurrant drink that I was after, but a bottle of Robinson's Barley Water.

'Look,' she said, 'are you in the drinks business or am I? I know perfectly well what a cordial is, and Robinson's Barley Water is a cordial.'

I told her that, as far as I knew, Robinson's was, and had been for generations, a fruit squash. If she insisted on referring to it as a cordial, that was fine by me, but I doubted if she was in the majority.

'I do insist,' she said, 'and we're out of it anyway. What's more, I shall be very surprised if you'll find a bottle of it anywhere in this weather.'

I told her that was the silliest thing I had ever heard, since there were obviously plenty of bottles of the stuff somewhere in London.

'You're welcome to go and look,' she said.

What is the point in arguing with the lower orders when they are in that sort of mood? Tried every other shop and off-licence in the area, only to discover there wasn't a bottle of it to be had anywhere.

I can only assume that, if all off-licences are as ill-informed as mine, people have simply stopped asking for it.

Sunday, June 25th

To Kent to introduce Amanda to Mother.

Arrived shortly before lunch to find that she had asked Denys Ramsden over for a drink to meet us. I have never really been able to look him in the eye ever since Mother claimed earlier this year that he had given her a French kiss. I know he's nearly eighty, but I wouldn't put it past him. It's the way he twiddles his moustache I don't trust. Things were going extremely well, with the compliments flying in all directions, and Denys twiddling, and much lively discussion about the weather and the traffic on the journey down, when Mother suddenly launched off into a long discourse on Nabokov's *Lolita*, a novel which, as far as I was aware, she had neither read nor heard of. Unless, of course, Denys has been trying to force his tastes on to her in addition to his tongue. At all events, she proceeded to outline the plot of this older man's passion for this very young girl in startling detail, and had I not had the presence of mind to suggest a stroll round the garden before lunch, I really believe things could have taken a very uncomfortable turn indeed. As it was, she spent most of lunch making pointed references to the difference in our ages. When she asked Amanda what she was hoping to do when she left school, I really felt she had gone too far, and after coffee I proposed an early return to town.

At least the cat didn't get a chance to sink its claws into Amanda's leg, a trick in which it appears to be encouraged by Mother who is even more besotted by the creature than she was when Nigel and Priscilla gave it to her last Christmas.

As we were getting into the car, Mother said, 'Do get Simon to bring you down again soon. It's been such fun.' Amanda replied, 'I certainly will.' as if she really meant it.

Glanced in my rear view mirror as we set off down the road and saw that Denys Ramsden had his arm round Mother's waist. I only hope that's as far as she allows him to go.

Apologized to Amanda for Mother's tactless behaviour. She said, 'I thought she was sweet. She reminds me of my grandmother.'

Just so long as we are not about to acquire a grandfather.

Only a week to go now before Beddoes leaves for Brussels. I have designed a small chart listing the seven remaining days which I shall tick off as BB Day (Beddoes to Brussels Day) approaches. Anything to make the time go quicker.

Monday, June 26th

Woke feeling unusually excited. For a moment or two I could not think why; then realized, of course, that today is the start of Wimbledon fortnight – an event in the sporting and social calendar that I always look forward to with keen anticipation. Every year I promise myself that I am going to get up a small party and spend a day there roaming the courts, eating strawberries and cream and watching the great stars in action, but somehow time always seems to fly by and before I know what, Harry Carpenter is previewing the fortnight on TV and discussing the seedings with Dan Maskell before I have had a chance to send off to the ticket office – wherever that may be.

Still, the BBC coverage is always so good and Dan's comments are invariably so sensible that I wonder anyone bothers to go at all. Not that anyone I know ever does.

Said as much to Amanda this evening. She replied, 'Oh, we always go every year. It's such a good opportunity to meet one's friends.'

I gather they make two trips – once during the first week and then again on mens' quarter-finals day. No mention I notice of my joining them. However, I have a feeling the chairman also takes people along for business reasons, so perhaps she assumes I will be in on one of those.

Only six days to BB Day.

Tuesday, June 27th

Five days to BB Day. The time cannot go fast enough for my liking.

Wednesday, June 28th

A dreadful night's sleep, thanks to the non-stop antics of Beddoes and his Islamic paramour. I do not often sleep with women but when I do, I certainly do not find it necessary to broadcast the fact to the entire neighbourhood.

Still wide awake at 1.30, so turned on my radio and listened for a while to an excellent Schubert concert from Holland. On the point of dozing off during slow movement of C Major Quintet when jerked back to life by loud hammering on the door and Beddoes's voice calling out, 'Would you mind turning off that terrible row? Some of us are trying to get to sleep.'

Finally got off shortly before three.

Overslept badly, leapt out of bed in panic and ricked my neck.

Felt so wretched all day, was quite unable to tackle Ruth re Barford figures or Roundtree re my new office.

To dinner with the Trubshawes. Amanda in excellent form and full of plans for party going, etc. Sadly incapable of joining in with any degree of enthusiasm. Enid most sympathetic about my neck and has arranged for me to see her man in Harley Street.

I have wasted far too much of my life hanging around bleak corridors in National Health hospital clinics, waiting for hours to see some apparently non-existent consultant before finally being fobbed off with an assistant. Time is money for a man in my position, and to deny oneself private medicine is short-sighted and uneconomic.

All other considerations apart, I cannot risk another journey on my scooter like this morning's when I was unable to look either to right or left and ended up being knocked over by a pedestrian in South Audley Street.

Four days to BB Day.

Thursday, June 29th

To Harley Street at noon. Place stiff with Arabs, largely of the brown-robed, scruffy-bearded variety. After waiting for ten minutes in a small, quite well-furnished room with a Peter Scott reproduction over the fireplace and a large pile of out-of-date copies of *Vogue* on the table, the receptionist arrived to say she was very sorry but Sheik Somebody-or-other had just flown in from the gulf with a slipped disc, and would I mind terribly hanging on for another quarter of an hour or so.

I may not be earning a thousand pounds a minute, but my time is not so worthless that I can afford to have it wasted at the whim of some rough Bedouin. Receptionist finally condescended to show me into large panelled consulting room.

Dr Andrews seemed a little too off-hand for a Harley Street man to my way of thinking, and when I introduced Enid's name into the proceedings, he seemed scarcely to remember her at all.

Am wondering if there might not be a hint of the Levant in Dr Andrews, if not the actual tarbrush.

He sat me in an upright chair, twisted my arms behind my back and started to manipulate me.

I remarked that it was a wonder people didn't finish up with broken necks.

one more nail in the coffin of the OF Society as far as I'm concerned.

Sunday, July 2nd

I can hardly believe that today is the last day I shall ever have to share my home or my life with Beddoes.

One would have thought he'd have enough to occupy himself with – packing suitcases, writing out cheques for his share of the household bills and generally making himself pleasant and useful around the place for once. But no. He has to devote the large part of his last day in this country lounging around in bed with Miss Teheran. Had been gearing myself up to a final outburst of noise, celebration and general bad behaviour on his part to such an extent that, even though he did not emerge from his room until half past three in the afternoon, I had exhausted myself with anticipation, and the tension had made my neck ache so badly that I had to take two Codein and lie down. I can't think of many people capable of upsetting others by doing nothing.

Finally got down to the Sunday papers just before supper.

By all accounts, I have missed absolutely nothing by not going to the first week of Wimbledon. Since I am still barely able to move my neck, let alone swivel it from side to side, I'm really quite glad the Trubshawes didn't ask me after all. I'd only have had to refuse.

Monday, July 3rd

Hurrah, hurrah. The day I have been looking forward to for so long and thought would never come.

Ralph Beddoes, my so-called flatmate for the past two and a half years, left these shores (or at any rate these rooms) at nine-thirty this morning, taking the ghastly Shusha, his beastly smelling cigars, his towelling dressing gown, his collection of pornographic magazines, and his irritating air of lecherous superiority with him.

The moment I saw him stepping into the taxi in the street below I rushed round the flat throwing open all the windows.

The one in his room had been closed for so long that I had quite a struggle shifting it, and when I did, it shot up to the top, breaking two panes, and would not come down again.

Even when he is not here, Beddoes costs me money. Still, a little broken glass is a small price to pay for the pleasure of feeling his presence blowing out through the window along with the months of accumulated dust. I shall send him the bill in Brussels. If he shows signs of dragging his heels over it, I shall have no hesitation in putting pressure on him through the appropriate government body here at Westminster. Which reminds me, I still haven't the faintest idea what he will be doing in Brussels. Neither, I suspect, does he.

Tuesday, July 4th

In the words of the song, I feel as corny as Kansas in August *and* as high as a flag on the Fourth of July. However, while I have nothing against Americans, ex-patriate or otherwise, celebrating their independence, I do draw a line at junior executives from Des Moines, Iowa, trying to teach me how to draw up a Barford New Product Development plan.

Miss Ruth Macmichael has tried to force-feed me with her slick Madison Avenue marketing methods just once too often. I am not by nature a vindictive man, but I must confess I took great pleasure this morning in slapping her down in no un-certain terms. I was disappointed that Roundtree should have seen fit to take her side in the matter, though not half as much as I was at Enid and Amanda setting off for the men's quarter-finals without so much as a mention of my joining them.

Wednesday, July 5th

Amanda came round after work to watch Wimbledon on the TV. Considering it was her first visit to my home since we met in May, and thus something of an historic occasion, I felt she might have shown a little more interest in the place. I had made quite an effort – hoovering right through, polishing the furniture, putting out a new roll of loo paper, etc.; yet when I asked her what she thought, all she said was, 'It's all right. Where's the TV set?'

A strangely incurious attitude towards her possible future home.

I also thought she made rather a meal about my not having

a colour set. In my view, one loses nothing in black and white, and as far as sport is concerned, the definition is, if anything, slightly sharper.

Despite the high standard of the men's doubles matches we were watching, she talked of nothing but Bjorn Borg. She seems positively obsessed by the fellow, and is evidently quite blind to his scruffy, rather bad-tempered appearance.

Eventually could not resist remarking that I was beginning to wish he had never been bjorn.

She stared at me blankly, so I repeated my little joke. She still didn't get it and I gave up. Later we watched a recording of a ladies' semi-final. I said that in my opinion Yvonne Goolagong was the most elegant player to have emerged since Maria Bueno.

'Who's Maria Bueno?' she asked.

The generation gap raises its ugly head at the most unexpected moments. One longs to bridge it, but how? I hardly know where to begin.

Vaguely at the back of my mind was the thought that we might celebrate the occasion by breaking the sexual ice. However, quickly realized the time was not right and scrapped the idea.

It never did anyone any harm to wait.

Thursday, July 6th

Men's semi-finals day at Wimbledon, but still not a word from the Trubshawes about my going with them. Returned to my desk after my usual ten o'clock visit to the coffee machine to find an envelope addressed to me in the unmistakable hand of Miss Ruth Macmichael. Scrawled across one corner was the word URGENT.

Decided I had had quite enough of these curt transatlantic business methods and tore the whole thing up without so much as a second glance.

Enjoyed a rare coup at lunchtime. Called into the delicatessen near the office and, after some deliberation, bought myself a piece of cold game pie. Astounded to be informed by sniffy, over-made-up girl at the cash desk that the modest slice I had chosen came to £1.30. In my confusion, handed over a single pound note, at which the girl gave me 70p in change. I suppose I should have said something, but I have never much cared for her manner, and it will do her no harm to take the rap.

Ate pie in square and afterwards fell asleep in the warm sun. Woke just before three and hurried back to the office, much refreshed. Spent a comparatively pleasant afternoon with the Barford figures and left promptly at five-thirty. Bumped into the chairman in the front hall who said, 'Hello, you're leaving it a bit late, aren't you?' I had no idea what he was talking about and said so. He frowned and said, 'You did get the ticket, didn't you? Miss Macmichael promised me faithfully she'd leave it on your desk in good time. Centre Court tickets are hard enough to come by at the best of times, but on men's semi-final day they're like gold dust.'

Rushed upstairs to my office to find that the cleaners had, for once, decided to empty the waste-paper baskets early.

Every bus crammed to bursting point, so did not arrive home until six-thirty by which time recording of afternoon's big games was over.

Consoled myself with thought that I could still watch it on Match of the Day. However, suddenly struck down by violent stomach upset and forced to retire to bed.

So much for game pie. I've a good mind to say something to that girl at the delicatessen.

Friday, July 7th

Woke feeling extremely queasy and decided to treat myself to a morning in bed for the first time in months. At least no-one can accuse me of hypochondria. Tried reading *Tess of the d'Urbervilles* for the umpteenth time and, as usual, failed to get beyond page two. Is it just me, or is Hardy a wildly over-rated novelist?

I doubt the so-called intellectuals would rate Ed McBain alongside the great masters of the written word, but at least one can get through his books at a sitting.

Saturday, July 8th

To the Trubshawes for lunch followed by the men's tennis finals. Try as I might I simply cannot warm to Bjorn Borg. I'm sure that, if one were to get to know him, one would discover that he is a quiet, simple lad, as capable of enjoying a pint and cracking a joke as the next fellow. Even so, I do not believe one can ever quite trust a man whose eyes are set so close together.

Sunday, July 9th

The day following some great sporting occasion inevitably brings with it a sense of deep anticlimax and today was no exception.

In an effort to liven up proceedings, invited Amanda to new Woody Allen film. How a girl with an expensive education like hers can have reached the age of eighteen without having seen one of Woody's films beats me. The prospect of trying to fill her in on the required background between The Boltons, Kensington and The Screen on the Hill, Belsize Park, was daunting to say the least.

Was perched in the drawing room at The Boltons, idly riffling through the new *Queen*, when the chairman stuck his head round the door and said he would like a short chat with me in his study. Naturally I assumed it had something to do with my new responsibilities at the office, so that when he asked me, 'What exactly are your intentions towards my daughter?' the wind was slightly taken out of my sails.

'I intend' I told him, 'to make her happy.'

He frowned impatiently and said, 'Yes yes, but how exactly?'

I was rather non-plussed by his line of questioning and said, 'I don't think I'm quite with you, Derrick.'

'It's quite simple,' he said. 'Are you or are you not planning to marry Amanda?'

I said that I was very much thinking along those lines.

'When?' he said. '2001?' – and left the room, tongue firmly in cheek I trust.

Amanda took so long getting ready that we were too late for the film and had to content ourselves with a sentimental piece of soap about tennis, called *Players*.

At least Bjorn Borg wasn't in it.

Monday, July 10th

Scooter on the blink again, so compelled to travel to work on the tube.

Arrived at the office in a rage and went straight to coffee

machine. What I had failed to notice in my nervous condition was that the stupid thing was out of plastic cups, so stuck my hand casually into pouring area only to have it scalded by a shower of boiling hot liquid. Managed to alleviate pain to some extent by plunging it immediately under nearby cold tap.

Was on my way back to the office when Armitage stalked past and made for the machine, a coin ready in his hand. Said nothing. Had just sat down at my desk when Ruth marched in without so much as a by-your-leave and asked if I had any comments on her suggestions for revising the Barford projected sales figures. She pointed at a green file on the top of my in-tray. I said I was afraid I had not had time to look at anything, and explained about my scalded hand.

'We all have our crosses to bear,' she said, 'and one of mine is that I have you as my Assistant Group Head. Frankly, if I were you, I'd get my ass out of the sling pretty damn quick.'

I was astounded by her insolence and would have replied that if anyone needed to get anyone's ass out of any sling it was hers, but I simply could not bring myself to utter the words. No sooner had she left than Armitage stuck his head round the door and said leeringly, 'Some people get all the luck.'

When I asked him what he meant, he replied, 'Who needs a group when you've got a piece of tail like that at your beck and call every day?'

And he winked suggestively and sipped noisily at a plastic beaker.

'Where did you get that?' I asked him.

'Out of the machine, of course,' he said, and with another loud laugh he walked off.

I do not give a fig for his opinions of Miss Macmichael, yet I have to admit, she is, for all her abrasive New York ways, strangely attractive. But then the way things are with Amanda at the moment, even Brenda from Accounts could set my loins ablaze.

Tuesday, July 11th

With Amanda and a group of her friends to see the new James Bond film. The most preposterous hotch-potch of gadgetry, sexual innuendo and over-acting I have ever wasted good money on in my life. Timmy and Joanna screamed with laughter throughout like a couple of excited school-children. Sorry to note that Amanda showed no less discrimination and joined in even more loudly. Dave, who has a stall in Camden Lock market, appeared to be the only one with the nous to see through it all.

As we were leaving he commented, 'Bloody immoral, that's what it is.'

I said that I quite agreed, and was reminiscing briefly about the great days of Sean Connery, Ursula Andress, Honor Blackman et al., when Dave interrupted me to say that it was not the morality he was complaining about but the cost. I said that, speaking as a practitioner in the communication business, I knew only too well the lengths to which one has to go these days to attract the public.

'No, no,' he said, interrupting me again. 'I meant the cost of the ticket.'

Business may not be booming at Camden Lock, but I noticed that did not prevent him from joining us for an expensive jumboburger at one of those ubiquitous, quasi-American fast-food joints that are so popular these days amongst the young, the ex-patriates and the indiscriminating.

Place full, hot and loud with pop music so that I could scarcely hear a word anyone said. Not that anyone had anything very interesting to say anyway – at least, not to me. Had barely placed our orders with a surly waitress with pink hair when Joanna said in a loud voice, 'Pooh, what an awful smell,' and Timmy said, 'I reckon someone's just let off.'

Noticed that there was a fat corgi asleep under the table of the couple next door.

Finally the smell became so bad that I leaned across and said to the owner, 'Excuse me, but I think your dog is suffering from flatulence.'

He put down his knife and fork, turned to me and said, 'If you must know, *I'm* suffering from flatulence.' To which his wife added, 'And I think it's jolly mean of you to draw attention to other people's medical conditions. How would you like it if I suddenly started shouting round the restaurant that you have bad breath?'

I said coolly, 'I do not happen to have bad breath, and if I did, I would certainly take care not to inflict it on innocent strangers in public places.'

'As a matter of interest,' said the man, 'you do have bad breath and it's putting me off my food.'

And with that they got up and left, taking their smelly Welsh dog with them. After they had gone, I said with a laugh, 'Talk about mote and beam.'

Amanda said, 'Actually, he was quite right; your breath is peculiarly pungent this evening.'

'Yes,' said Joanna. 'In fact, I thought the smell came from you.'

Needless to say, they did not get much change out of me for the rest of the evening.

Wednesday, July 12th

The morning post brings Dr Andrews's bill for dealing with my neck. Forty guineas, if you please.

As soon as I got to the office I rang Harley Street and pointed out to the secretary that whoever it was who made out the bills was obviously labouring under the misapprehension that I had been there twice.

'If you must know,' she said tartly, 'I made out your bill and, unlike you, I am not suffering from anything. One consultation with Dr Andrews – forty guineas. We have made a slight reduction in consideration of your relationship with the Trubshawe family. However, we'd be quite happy to waive this, if you would prefer it.'

I replied that I was simply checking and put the phone down. Thank heavens for my private patients' scheme, that's all I can say.

Thursday, July 13th

Rang the private patients people in Eastbourne to ask them to send me a claim form.

Spoke to a Miss Hart who asked me when I had seen my own doctor. I told her that I had gone straight to the specialist.

'Oh,' she said, 'I'm afraid we cannot contemplate a claim unless we have a statement from your own doctor saying that he recommended the treatment in question.'

I pointed out that when one is suffering from a stiff neck, one does not need a doctor to tell one what is wrong or what to do about it.

She said, 'That may be your opinion, but I'm afraid we're quite firm on this point.'

I decided the time had come to read the riot act to Miss Hart and did so.

When I had finished she said, 'What is your name again?' I told her. There was a brief pause, then she came on the line again.

'I'm sorry, Mr Crisp,' she said, 'but according to our records you cancelled your subscription last November.'

And just as well, if this is the standard of service one can expect from private medicine nowadays.

Friday, July 14th

Le quartorze juillet as our neighbours on the other side of the Channel have it. I do not hold much of a brief for the French, especially in the light of their high-handed behaviour towards us in the EEC. On the other hand, for all their rudeness and over-eating and smelly cigarettes, they are very much of a piece as a nation. Their policemen do not drive round on German motorbikes, nor does one hear the phrase '*société multiraciale*' being bandied round smart Parisian dinner tables. It's a pity *we* do not set aside a special day every year when we can express our pride in our nation with eating and drinking and dancing in the streets. That way we might feel more confident about putting our so-called *confrères* in their proper place at the conference tables of Brussels and Strasbourg. It might also do something towards improving the standard of food in motorway cafés.

Saturday, July 15th

At somewhat of a loose end, as Amanda has agreed to go down to the Hamble for the weekend with Enid and help choose fabrics for the saloon of the yacht which they are having redecorated at huge expense.

We seem to see less and less of each other these days. Still, that may not be such a bad thing. Familiarity *does* breed contempt, and it never pays for two young people to be constantly on top of each other. Not that we ever are, of course, but there's plenty of time for all that sort of thing in due course.

Am seriously thinking of asking Ruth out to lunch next

week with a view to clearing the air and re-establishing the lines of communication. Meanwhile, decided to improve the shining hour by walking up to Kensington High Street and buying myself a new pair of underpants from one of the large stores. Found the perfect pair in dark blue with red piping. Asked the girl for a pair in medium, but was told they only had them in small and large. I suggested she might care to look in the stock drawer before coming out with such a definitive statement.

She said, 'I don't have to look in the stock drawer to know that we only have those in small and large.'

I pointed out that, if that was true, it was extremely bad marketing on the part of the store, since the majority of male customers took medium.

'I know,' she said, 'That's why we've only got small and large left in stock.'

I replied that frankly I did not believe her and suggested she called for the floor walker. After a long wait, a young man came hurrying up, all teeth and smiles and rimless glasses, to explain that they were expecting a new supply of mediums in on Monday.

I said, 'Do you absolutely promise me they will be here? I have to come from quite a long way specially.'

He said, 'You have my word.' For what that's worth.

Sunday, July 16th

I'm sorry now that I didn't take a pair of the plain light blue since I discover this morning that I am completely out of clean underpants altogether. However, my bathing trunks will act as a perfectly satisfactory substitute until tomorrow.

Devoted most of the morning to washing out a few shirts and socks and the afternoon to cleaning the car. There's no more healthy therapy than manual labour, even if it does give you chapped skin.

Monday, July 17th

Lunch hour given over entirely to collecting underpants. Incredibly, they were still out of mediums. Demanded to see the floor walker.

'Can you remember his name?' the assistant asked me.

I told her that we had not been introduced. After a certain amount of to-ing and fro-ing, a quite different young man appeared from the nether regions to say that they had been expecting the mediums in at eleven o'clock that morning, but that there had been a hold-up with the van. I reminded him that I was promised they would be there, which was why I had given up my valuable free time to come all that way. 'Not by me, you weren't,' said the young man.

I suppose I could have kicked up a real stink if I'd wanted, but in the end said I'd settle for a pair of the plain pale blue.

'We sold the last one of those on Saturday morning,' he said. I suppose the white ones are really just as good and, as the young man pointed out, as long as they do their job what difference does it make what colour they are?

Tried them on this evening after supper only to discover a small hole in a most awkward place. Why is it that one has to go shopping twice for everything these days?

Bang goes my lunch date with Ruth tomorrow.

Tuesday, July 18th

Ruth surprisingly nice about my cancelling our tête-à-tête. Although she said it was all the same by her, there was no disguising the disappointment in her voice. Have suggested dinner tomorrow night instead and she has accepted. It won't do her any harm to be on tenterhooks for another 36 hours.

A pity someone doesn't think up a way of keeping shop assistants a bit more on their toes. First of all the girl pretended she couldn't see where the hole was, and when she did finally admit its existence, she peered at it for a moment, then said, 'Are you sure you're not to blame?'

I did not care for her implications one little bit and I'm afraid we had sharp words about it.

However, in the end she agreed, rather grudgingly, to let me take another pair. I also bought some socks while I was about it. Dark blue, rather nice.

Wednesday, July 19th

Amanda rang this morning to say she had been asked to a charity dress show and did I want to go? I explained about my previous engagement with Ruth in as tactful a way as possible but got no reaction. I'd have expected her to show some sign of jealousy. Called Ruth just before lunch to ask where she'd like to dine. She said, 'Oh, is it tonight? I'd quite forgotten. Actually I've just agreed to go to Covent Garden. Can we make it another time?'

I was astounded at her casual attitude and made my feelings felt. But all she said was, 'I didn't realize it was such a big deal. I thought it was just an informal business reappraisal.'

I said stiffly, 'It all depends on how much of a big deal you think your career is,' and quietly put the phone down.

The maddening thing is, I was actually rather looking forward to it all. But I'm certainly not going to let her know that.

Rang Amanda to say I would be free for the dress show after all.

'Oh, that's a pity,' she said coolly, 'I've arranged to go with Colin.' Suppose she must mean Armitage, but didn't labour the point. The prospect of him and me becoming relations is too awful to contemplate.

Thursday, July 20th

Mother rang this evening to ask me if I'd remembered Priscilla's birthday on Saturday. I hadn't, as it happened, any more than my sister remembers mine, and to be reminded of the fact makes me even less willing to do anything about it.

Really, the sooner Mother stops treating me like a small child, the better for both our sakes. As I was leaving with Amanda the other day, I'll swear I heard her asking me if I had a clean handkerchief.

Friday, July 21st

Arrived in the office to find a note from Ruth saying that she hoped I wasn't planning anything elaborate for this evening, since she was lunching with the Barford New Product people. This is the first I've heard of it. If anyone should be lunching with anyone round here it should be me. Rang Roundtree and kicked up a stink, only to be informed that it was his idea, that Alec Giles was very partial to a pretty face, and that any company in this day and age that did not put itself out to make its client feel loved and wanted needed its head examined.

I didn't like to say so, but there are one or two people I can think of who need *their* heads examined. Including me. Am I a Group Head or aren't I? I understand now how poor old Wavell must have felt in the desert in 1941. Added the word INSUBORDINATION to my list of matters to be discussed this evening.

Went to put on new socks this evening and big toe went straight through the end. Not surprisingly, arrived at Bordelino in a fury. Also rather later than I had said. No sign of Ruth. Mentally added UNRELIABILITY to the list.

I must have eaten at that restaurant a score of times over the last couple of years, yet the head waiter appeared not to recognize me at all. However, when I mentioned my name he said, 'Ah yes, of course,' and began to scan the book.

'Your table was for eight-thirty,' he said.

'I know,' I said. 'I booked it myself. The corner one.'

'It is quarter to nine,' he said.

I said, laughingly, 'In my book, eight-thirty means anything between eight-thirty and nine o'clock.'

'Really,' he said, 'in mine it means anything between eight-thirty and eight-thirty!'

The upshot of this absurd exchange was that he had assumed we were not coming and had given the table away. However, if I cared to wait . . . ?

I replied stiffly that I did not care to do anything, least of all eat in his restaurant, and was on the point of leaving when Ruth arrived, looking, I must admit, very glamorous in a red velvet trouser suit.

To my astonishment, she and the waiter rushed at each other and embraced warmly, showering each other with compliments of a most intimate kind.

Frankly I felt a bit of a fool standing there, though not half as much as I did when 'Franco' rushed us to the best table in the house, muttering inanities like 'If I'd known it was you, *cara mia* . . .' and similar twaddle.

If there's one thing I dislike more than an obsequious head waiter it is an obsequious Italian head waiter. They're so *obvious*. As it turned out, though, dinner could not have been a greater success. I do not believe I have enjoyed myself so much for years. We hardly mentioned the office at all, and my list remained firmly in my pocket throughout.

Bill rather larger than I had anticipated; however, I shall almost certainly be able to claim it back on expenses.

As we stepped into the street Ruth said, 'Your place or mine then?'

Was momentarily thrown off balance by the bluntness of her approach, but quickly recovered my composure and said innocently, 'Oh, I think I've had enough coffee for one evening.'

'Who said anything about coffee, dum-dum?' she replied.

I said, 'I'm afraid I don't quite follow you.'

'What's there to follow?' she said. 'Do you want to fool around or don't you?'

One reads about this sort of thing happening in certain types of American literature, and I'd be the first to admit that there have been moments when I have day-dreamed about receiving such a proposition myself.

All I can say is that the fictional characters who take women up on those sort of offers (a) are obviously never feeling under the weather, (b) do not have to get up and go to work in the mornings, and (c) don't go out on dinner dates on their scooters.

On the other hand, I must confess I was not indifferent to her suggestion, and certainly did not want to close the door on it completely.

'I've heard about romance in the office,' I said with a laugh, 'but this is ridiculous.'

I suppose I should have realized that, like all Americans, Ruth has very little sense of humour.

'Thanks for nothing,' she said, and began to walk off down the street.

Decided to play things casually and called after her, 'I'll call you a cab.'

'Call me what you like,' she shouted over her shoulder, 'I only live a couple of blocks away.' And with a wave she disappeared from sight.

Though not perhaps a successful conquest in the accepted sense, I have a feeling I may have done myself more good than it may appear.

Saturday, July 22nd

How glad I am to have given up jogging when I did. Holland Park seems to have been turned into one vast cross-country running course. At every turn one is confronted by yet another sweating, red-faced fanatic, heaving his unhealthy bulk along on pink and white flabby legs, coughing, spitting, panting and generally spoiling the beauty and tranquillity of this historic preserve. Do people have no sense of place? If they want to do that sort of thing there are plenty of running tracks set aside for the purpose. I am seriously thinking of starting up an anti-jogging campaign. I can see it already: public meetings in Kensington Town Hall, articles in the paper, interviews on the 'Today' programme with Brian Redhead (or better still, Libby Purves), questions in Parliament, compulsory wording on every pair of gym shoes sold – JOGGING CAN BE HARMFUL TO YOUR HEALTH'. There's no end to it. Moreover, it's a well known fact that there is no better way of making one's name these days than by taking up some popular cause. Look at Peter Hain. His name is a household word. And Mahatma Gandhi. Who had ever heard of him before he took up non-violence?

Half expected Ruth to ring all evening.

She probably hasn't got my number.

Sunday, July 23rd

Still nothing from Ruth. Or from anyone else, come to that. Was walking in Holland Park again this afternoon following a morning of heavy rain. Stepped out of the way to avoid an on-coming jogger only to discover I had put my foot straight into a dog dirt. In those wet conditions it was indistinguishable from the surrounding mud.

Spent several minutes trying to wipe it off and was heading towards the car park when a large labrador jumped out of a Volvo and bounded towards me. I stood to one side, assuming it was setting out for a walk, but instead of rushing by, it leapt straight up at me with its dirty paws and slobbering jaws and then rushed back to the car, leaving my fawn trousers completely covered in black mud. I picked them up from the cleaners only yesterday.

Am thinking of changing my cause from anti-jogging to

anti-dogs. To judge by the state of the London pavements, I think it would do me every bit as much good.

Supper on a tray in front of the TV, again. How lonely it is in the flat these days. I never thought the day would come when I would actually miss Beddoes' presence.

Life is strange.

Monday, July 24th

I give up. Not only am I still no nearer to getting a new office, but I arrived this morning to find that over the week-end someone has seen fit to substitute my homely, if somewhat cigarette-scarred, wooden desk for a metal monstrosity half the size.

Not only that, but Miss Macmichael even more difficult and insulting about my Barford projections than ever.

I said that the mood of *détente* achieved on Friday night appeared to have been constructed very much on shifting sand.

'Friday night was pleasure,' she replied sharply, 'or rather it might have been. Today it's back to business as usual.'

So I see.

It's interesting that the most attractive women are also frequently the most ruthless. It would make an excellent subject for a thesis. Or even a book. The *Sunday Times* would snap it up like a shot. If they weren't on strike that is.

Took sub-standard socks back to shop and had further words with buyer. I may very well refer the matter to a higher authority.

Tuesday, July 25th

By one of those coincidences that are almost too astonishing to be true, I opened the paper in the tube this morning to find an advertisement for something called the Creative Writing Academy, with an address in South London.

'ARE YOU THE NEW SOMERSET MAUGHAM?' demanded the headline. 'How do you know unless you try?' continued the sub-heading.

If the copy is to be believed, by the simple device of giving up the equivalent of one evening's TV viewing time a week,

I can learn how to write and sell TV and film scripts, newspaper articles, short stories, even novels.

Have written off for the free booklet *Writing for Money*, enclosing a brief letter explaining that I have already completed half a novel while at Oxford, and that although one or two of my friends at the time commented that it was far too obviously based on Evelyn Waugh, I could not see it myself and still cannot. I agree that *Brideshead Revisited* is a very good book in its way, but that does not necessarily put all novels about undergraduate life completely out of bounds. I do not know how this will go down with the Director of Studies, but I wanted to make it clear to whoever runs the course that I am not a complete beginner.

Wednesday, July 26th

On my way in to work on the tube this morning, found myself reading *Daily Telegraph* with an altogether fresher and more critical eye. At one point, got out Pentel and found myself instinctively correcting an article about Norman St John Stevas. Also jotted down a few notes for a short story. I have long suspected that beneath this hard commercial exterior lies a deeply creative nature.

Over coffee read an interesting, though not very well written, article bemoaning the fact that TV is spoiling cricket, and that to get the real feel and atmosphere of the game one must be there in person.

I quite agree.

As one who was privileged to see the great Cyril Washbrook come out of retirement to score 98 against the Australians at Leeds in 1956 but who these days prefers the easy option of the armchair in front of the TV set to the real thing, I am only too aware of the short-comings of the medium and long for the noise and smell and excitement that are the very warp and woof of this great British institution.

By a happy coincidence, the Second Test starts at Lord's tomorrow and I think I owe it to myself, both as a sportsman and a writer, to slip up there for the day.

Informed Roundtree that I should not be in, due to dentist appointment.

He said, 'That's all right. Ruth is quite capable of making those changes for the sales conference charts we discussed.'

I said nothing. What is the point? It is impossible to fault her in his eyes. I'm beginning to wonder if he might not be having a bit of a thing with her.

Thursday, July 27th

To Lord's for the Test Match.

Paid my entrance fee at one of the side gates and made my way to the Warner Stand, to which John Arlott and others are constantly referring, only to discover that a further charge of nearly three pounds was being asked. I told the official that, as far as I was concerned, I had already paid my entrance.

'Not to the Warner Stand, you haven't,' he replied.

'There are plenty of free seats at the Nursery End, you know.'

I said that this was the first I had heard of it and that in my view it was a pity this fact was not more widely and clearly advertised.

Made my way to the Nursery End, but had no sooner taken my seat than the umpire drew stumps for lunch.

En route for a beer and a sandwich, bumped into Armitage who said, 'I'd rather you didn't mention in the office that you've seen me here. I'm supposed to be at home, working on the Morton-Johnson figures.'

I've suspected for some time now that his position in the firm is shaky, to say the least, and now I'm sure of it.

After lunch, found a seat at the very front in the sun, and settled down to the afternoon's play.

It's really most interesting to see the great stars of modern cricket in the flesh after watching them for so many years on TV. Somehow they assume much more human proportions.

Also interested to note how much smaller Lord's is in real life. One really does miss these details on TV.

Not perhaps the most exciting afternoon's cricket; indeed at one point, nodded off for quite fifteen minutes.

All in all, though, I wouldn't have missed it for anything.

Friday, July 28th

Bumped into Roundtree on my way back from the coffee machine this morning. He said, 'I didn't realize they'd taken up dentistry at cricket matches.'

Assumed that Armitage had ratted on me, and feigned innocence.

'Come off it,' said Roundtree. 'I know you were at Lord's yesterday afternoon.'

'Lord's?' I exclaimed.

'People lie, but cameras don't,' he said. 'We were having a client meeting with the Morton-Johnson people in the chairman's office yesterday afternoon when David Johnson asked if he could see the Test score. We switched on the TV and there you were, large as life and twice as natural, in the front row of the public stands. And you were asleep.'

I replied that the standard of TV outside broadcast camera work is not so perfect that it is not capable of distorting the odd face from time to time, and walked away with dignity.

My problem now is whether to mention the matter to the chairman or say nothing. Silence certainly did Jeremy Thorpe's case no harm, and it can do me none to follow his example.

Have made a few more notes on my short story. It's shaping up well.

Saturday, July 29th

Slept collarless for the first time in weeks and feel all the better for it.

Lunched *chez* Trubshawe. As coffee was being poured Derrick announced he was off to his study to watch the Test Match on TV. He turned to me and said, 'Care to join me? I understand you're quite a keen cricket fan.' To have denied it or refused might have led to a confrontation, so I said, 'Yes, I am quite,' and followed him from the room.

He did not refer again directly to my enthusiasm for the game, but I am sure he is *au courant* with my escapade in St John's Wood. All very embarrassing and awkward. According to Mollie Marsh-Gibbon, TV companies are legally bound to pay a fee of five pounds to anyone who appears, however fleetingly, in any of their programmes. I may very well take the matter up with the BBC. In the meantime, I have more pressing and delicate matters to attend to, not least of which is knocking my story into shape. It is called 'Dog', which the other way round spells God.

Sunday, July 30th

I have been thinking. I have no alternative but to tender my resignation to Roundtree tomorrow morning. It is the only honourable course open to me.

Story going less well today. I think I may be suffering from writer's block.

Mentioned it to Amanda who said, 'Housemaid's knee more likely.' Has she really got what it takes to be a writer's wife, I ask myself?

Monday, July 31st

Spent most of the day wrestling with my letter of resignation. I know now what Anthony Eden must have gone through in 1938.

Armitage stuck his head round the door later and said, in a suggestive tone of voice, 'If you have any problems with my cousin, just let me know.'

I told him that would not be necessary.

What *has* Amanda been saying to him? I have never really trusted cousins ever since reading *Rebecca*.

August

Tuesday, August 1st

A truly extraordinary coincidence. Was on my way out of the office to deliver my letter to Roundtree when the phone rang. It was the Barford marketing chap, Neville Pratt, wanting to know if I was at all interested in changing jobs, because, if so, he had a proposition he wanted to put to me. I could hardly believe my ears. However, I have always held that it never pays in business to express unqualified enthusiasm over anything, so have merely said I'd be interested to hear more, and we have arranged to lunch at the Ritz. I have always said Barfords is a company that's not afraid to spend money when necessary. Was tempted in my excitement to tear my letter of resignation into tiny pieces and scatter them over Ruth Macmichael, but sanity prevailed and I put it quietly away in a drawer. One never knows.

Wednesday, August 2nd

As we were leaving the Bordelino this evening after a difficult dinner, Amanda suddenly put her arms round my neck, gave me a smacking kiss and said, 'You're a funny old thing, but I do rather love you.'

Am not sure whether to be pleased or not.

Thursday, August 3rd

A day of decisions for which I dress accordingly in dark grey.

Great hotels like the Ritz have a way of bringing out the best in one, and as I entered the restaurant, I noticed that more than one person looked across in my direction. The fact that the head waiter had never even heard of Mr Pratt, or of Barfords, slightly spoilt the effect. However, all was explained a few moments later when Pratt arrived, full of apologies, with a colleague named Keith Hardacre. We went straight to the bar where Pratt had a large vodka and tonic, Keith had a large whisky and water, and I had a small Campari and soda, a drink that is lively without being too alcoholic.

'Not a serious drinking man, then?' Keith asked with a laugh. I said that I could be on occasions, but that I preferred to keep a clear head at lunchtime.

'Sensible man,' said Keith, swallowing his whisky. 'Another one for you, Nev?'

Neville said, 'Hold your horses, Keith,' swallowed his vodka and banged his empty glass down on the table.

Keith looked at me and said, 'Simon?'

I shook my head politely.

'Sensible fellow,' said Keith, and nodded at Pratt who nodded back, and they both nodded at a passing waiter and ordered another round of the same.

After that they had another round and then we went in to lunch, and a first-class lunch it was too. Barfords certainly know how to push the boat out.

I drank one glass of white wine and one of red. Keith and Neville got through the best part of a bottle each, and yet, apart from the moment when Keith tipped a spoonful of *petits pois* into his lap, it seemed to have no effect on them.

When the coffee came, Keith said, 'Liqueur, Simon? Cognac? Tia Maria?'

I said I wouldn't have anything.

'Sensible chappie,' said Keith. 'Nev?'

They both ordered large Green Chartreuses on the rocks. We then got down to business.

Keith, who is a director of Barfords and Neville's boss, did the talking. The idea apparently is that I should join them in a PR sort of capacity, as a kind of roving ambassador, travelling here and there and generally handling the corporate image of Barfords. It all sounds most exciting and very much my sort of style, and when they mentioned the salary (£12,000 a year) I nearly fell off my seat. That's half as much again as I am getting at Harley Preston.

Talk about offers one can't refuse.

It is high time I got out and about a bit in the world before married life pins me down once and for all. Like T. S. Eliot, I could easily fit my writing in in the evenings and at weekends.

Was quite tempted to say 'yes' and be done with it. On the other hand, it will be interesting to see the lengths to which Harley Preston are prepared to go to keep me on, and I said I would let them know in a few days. 'Sensible fellow,' said Keith, and we all had a celebratory Green Chartreuse which made me feel rather sick.

As we were shaking hands on the steps, Keith said in an earnest sort of way, 'Do join us,' and gave my hand an odd little squeeze.

I had the distinct feeling he was trying to tell me something. Walked back to the office in the warm sunshine in a strangely puzzled mood.

Friday, August 4th

Once one has made up one's mind to a thing, there is no point in prolonging the agony and I pinned Roundtree down to a confrontation at 3.15. I cut the chit-chat and came straight to the point. 'I think I should tell you,' I told him, 'that I have been offered a post at Barfords at £12,000 a year. I'd be interested to hear what you have to say.'

'Congratulations,' Roundtree said.

I said, 'So you're not interested in matching the offer?'

'No,' he said.

'I see,' I said. 'Still, I daresay you'd like me to work out my notice. As you know, I have quite a bit on at present.'

He said, 'I don't think that will be necessary. Ruth pretty well knows the form by now.'

I was, and still am, dumbfounded. For two pins I'd leave tomorrow.

Unfortunately I have not yet received an official letter from Barfords offering me the job. Am hoping Roundtree will not mention the matter to Derrick for a day or two, just in case.

Rang Neville's office to be told he was in Leeds. Keith Hardacre also away. Had a row with Ruth and went home early.

Have decided to scrap short story in favour of a novel about a man who suddenly at the age of 36 decides to change his job. It's coming along rather well.

Saturday, August 5th

Surprised and disappointed to have heard nothing yet from the Creative Writing people. However, novel going so well I'm beginning to wonder if I'm really going to need the course after all.

Amanda rang to ask me to Joanna and Timmy's party, but I pleaded pressure of work.

She said, 'You never want to do anything any more. I don't know why we bother to go on.'

I pointed out that relationships with writers have always been notoriously difficult and quoted as examples Byron and Hardy.

She said, 'I don't know about Hardy, but at least Byron was sexy.'

I said that if a cripple who was mad, bad and dangerous to know was her idea of sexy, then I gave up.

'Yes,' she said. 'It is.'

I reminded her that sex appeal and literary talent were totally unconnected; the whole point was that one could not afford to be distracted by trivial social activities, adding that it was well known that, when Nancy Mitford was writing a book, she never saw anyone for weeks on end.

She said. 'Don't say you're changing sex. That would explain everything.'

And she rang off.

All very distressing, but as a writer one will have to learn to live with this kind of thing.

Sunday, August 6th

Damn and blast it. I've missed Glyndebourne again. Every year I promise myself I will join the dinner-jacketed revellers on the famous afternoon train, hamper in one hand, a pretty girl in the other. I have never cared a lot for opera. On the other hand, the idea of wandering around the lawns of a country house, sipping champagne in the cool of a summer's evening in the company of Bernard Levin, Arianna Stassinopoulos and others has always appealed to me, and to have never experienced it is surely to have missed one of the essential pleasures of English life as we know it. Or don't, in my case.

I wonder if I shouldn't try and work it into my novel in some way?

I'm thinking of calling it *The Long Look Back*, but may change it later.

Monday, August 7th

Lunched with Mollie Marsh-Gibbon in what she described as the best fish restaurant in London and turned out to be nothing more than a glorified fish and chip shop. Wandsworth is a long way to go for the doubtful pleasure of deep-fried hake. I'm not surprised that very few people know about it. Still, one can't tell Mollie anything, and I didn't try.

True to form, she was most scornful of my lunch at the Ritz, saying that only jumped-up media people and second-rate estate agents ever eat there nowadays. When I mentioned the curious handshake Keith had given me, she shrieked, 'My dear fellow, don't you know anything? The chap's obviously a Mason. I'd steer clear of that firm if I were you.'

I had neither the time nor the inclination to take her up on the matter, but her comments have certainly set me thinking. Perhaps Keith *was* inviting me to become a fellow Mason, and is waiting for me to take him up on this before he will commit himself to offering me the job officially. But how to find out for certain? This is one of those tricky little situations one meets from time to time in one's professional life and which, if handled badly, can lead to disaster.

First things first: I must do a bit of research into this whole subject of Freemasonry.

Curiously enough, I have always been very interested to know what it's all about, and this is an excellent opportunity to find out at last.

Tuesday, August 8th

I have never really had a lot of truck with astrology, and when I skim through the horoscope in my newspaper every morning, I treat it very much as I treat theatre and cinema reviews – as good entertainment but not to be taken too literally.

However, this morning the forecast for the weekend reflects my life with an accuracy that is surely more than coincidental.

'This could turn out to be one of the most outstanding weekends of your life, and one of the happiest. Forge ahead confidently with everything you are doing at present, and take care to accept every invitation you are offered. Refusal at this stage could cause you much unhappiness in the long run.'

It's almost as if the writer is thoroughly *au fait* with the most intimate details of my life. I wonder if it's anyone I know?

Wednesday, August 9th

To the Westminster Public Library to consult the standard history of Freemasonry by Brother Ellis. Most interested to discover that there is scarcely a great man in history who was *not* a Mason: Christopher Wren, George Washington, Robert Burns, Mozart, Edward VII. Were I to join, I should obviously be in good company, and I have no doubt I am as well fitted to become a member of a lodge as the next man. I am over 21, a free man of good report and integrity, and would certainly come of my own free will. On the other hand, do I really want to become a Lodge Master, or an Inner Guard, or even a Junior Deacon? A writer's life is full enough as it is.

Indeed, if Brother Ellis's report is anything to go by, it is going to take all my time just to grasp the fundamental principles of Freemasonry. I have no first-hand experience of the building industry, and lines like 'We cannot properly consider the square without associating it with Euclid's 47th Proposition' set my mind reeling.

I am also suspicious of this connection with Solomon's Temple. I'm wondering if the Jews have a hand in it somewhere.

Frankly, after an hour's concentrated reading, I am as baffled as ever. So, I daresay, are the large majority of Masons, if they would but admit it. What an intelligent fellow like Mozart saw in it all is beyond me.

On the other hand, I think I would be unwise to dismiss the whole idea willy-nilly. I am not a superstitious man, but my horoscope was quite specific on the subject of invitations, and for the moment I intend to reserve judgement.

Thursday, August 10th

Still nothing from Barfords. Morning spent in an agony of doubt and indecision. Other considerations apart, if I don't receive confirmation of my new job soon, I shall seriously have to consider taking lodgers. I really cannot afford to keep this flat going at this rate.

After lunch, could stand suspense no longer and rang Keith's secretary, Miss Hippo. Said who I was and explained that I had been away for a few days and that I was just ringing to find out if by chance he had been trying to get in touch with me. She said, 'No. Why, should he have been?' I said, 'Not really.' She said, 'Mr Hardacre is a very busy man. Why should he ring for no reason?'

I said, 'It was just that he'd promised to let me have some information about a club he belongs to.'

'Club?' said Miss Hippo. 'What sort of a club?'

I told her it was not exactly a club, more a society. She said she was not aware of his belonging to any societies. I said in a confidential tone of voice, 'It has loose connections with architecture, or more precisely the building industry, if you know what I mean.'

Miss Hippo said, 'I can only suggest that I pass the message on to Mr Hardacre and let him come back to you in person.' And before I could stop her, she had put the phone down on me.

I hope the secretaries at Barfords are not as hopeless at passing on messages as Sarah is in our office.

Friday, August 11th

Was on my way to the coffee machine this morning when Keith rang and said, 'I understand from my secretary that you are interested in joining the National Trust. This is excellent news. We need as many members as we can get. I've asked them to send you all the requisite bumph. You should be getting it any day now. Must dash.' And he rang off.

Curiously enough I have often considered the possibility of joining the National Trust.

Saturday, August 12

The 'Glorious Twelfth' indeed, since the morning post brings a fat manilla envelope from the Creative Writing people. As well as the booklet *Writing for Money*, there are various vouchers and a free copy of *The Moon and Sixpence*. Are they somehow in league with the Maugham family, one asks one-self?

Also included is a personal letter addressed 'Dear Writer' from the Director of Studies, Mr Brian Silver. I seem to have heard that name somewhere before. What he has to say is certainly to the point: the secret of successful writing is simply knowing *what* to write, and *how* to write.

Skimmed through *Writing for Money* which, among other things, contains letters from satisfied and successful students. One read: 'I have had two articles accepted by a gourmet magazine. . . . My life has been completely transformed. . . . I owe it all to the Creative Writing Course.' Signed H.B-F. London.

If that isn't Hugh Bryant-Fenn I'll eat my hat. If he's an example of one of their successes, I'd hate to think where their failures wind up.

At all events, have decided to accept their free trial offer to read and criticize any piece of descriptive writing of no more than 500 words that I care to send within the next twenty-one days. Oddly enough, I have had the feeling for several days now that I am about to give birth to an outburst of creativity.

After much agonizing, settled for a walk in Richmond Park beneath the shade of the beeches – alone, of course. Set off after lunch. A perfect summer's afternoon: warm and sunny with just the faintest hint of a breeze kissing the panting grass. Above, an azure sky was decorated with tiny puffs of white cloud, like blobs of cotton wool on a child's painting.

Butterflies lolloped from wild flower to wild flower, pausing briefly to sip at the warm honey before skipping on their way, while deep in the woods, turtle doves cooed seductively to the dozing deer. An English summer at its very best. . . .

Cut across towards Thatched Lodge, home of the Ogilvys. Slithered down the steep bank below the house and crossed the road. Was strolling happily through the thick bracken when I heard a strange sound away to my left, as though an animal were in pain.

Tip-toed towards the sound and hid behind a tree. Peered round the trunk to discover, as I thought, a young man in the process of murdering a young girl. Moved forward to protest when I suddenly realized that they were half naked and making love. Understandably I was frozen to the spot for a moment or two with embarrassment. Unfortunately, befor-I had a chance to move away, the girl spotted me and cried out, 'Bugger off, you dirty old man.' Was thinking I'd seen her before somewhere, when the man looked up.

I could scarcely believe my eyes. It was Colin Armitage. The girl, I suddenly realized, was Roundtree's secretary, Felicity. I do not believe I have been more shocked and embarrassed in my life. At the same time I was oddly excited, and all I could think about as I walked back to the car was how much I wanted to see Amanda. For two pins I'd have gone round to The Boltons there and then were I not so anxious to get the story down on paper while the events were still fresh in my mind. As a writer, one cannot afford to let such moments of inspiration pass and be dissipated in the pursuit of bodily gratification.

Finally settled down at the Olympia portable at six and worked on till Starsky and Hutch. Am experiencing some problems with the opening, but then even Maugham was prepared to sit all morning staring at a blank sheet of paper. The hardest thing of all is the title. I may call it *Summer Madness*.

Sunday, *August 13th*

Woke exhausted and disturbed after a restless night. At one point had a strangely erotic dream of a vaguely pornographic nature, concerning a member of the royal family. As a result, quite unable to settle to any serious work all day. Have definitely decided to change the title, though to what I am not as yet sure.

After supper watched 'Face the Music'. Lord Norwich, Mother's favourite, not on. Have come to the conclusion that there is only one item I dislike more than the Funny Opera and that's the Dummy Keyboard. Tonight they had both.

Monday, August 14th

The morning's post brings the long-awaited letter from Keith, officially offering me the job and laying down the conditions of employment. I am to be known as Deputy Marketing Manager, with direct responsibility to Neville Pratt, at a salary of £12,000 per annum, payable monthly as usual, and I am to begin as soon as my present commitments will allow. No further mention, I notice, of Freemasonry. Immediately drafted a letter of acceptance. The key to success in business is recognizing opportunities when they arise and seizing them with both hands. As Sir Freddie Laker said in a recent TV interview, re his executives: one can tolerate almost any fault except indecision. Spoke to Roundtree about date of leaving and have told him I am prepared to stay on for a further week. There are still one or two odds and ends to be tidied up and besides, there are many who would feel most aggrieved and hurt if I were to leave before they'd had a chance for a whip-round.

Sarah will almost certainly wish to organize some sort of farewell do in the pub.

Worked on my piece in the evening. I'm calling it *Summer Sonata*.

Tuesday, August 15th

Woke early and put finishing touches to the piece. It is faintly reminiscent of H. E. Bates. Decided to treat myself to small celebratory lunch at my favourite Greek restaurant near the office and posted Barford letter en route.

Was on way out when I felt a hand on my arm. Turned to find Bryant-Fenn reaching out from a table by the door, and inviting me to join him for a drink. He told me he was there in his capacity as restaurant critic for this much-heralded news magazine which is supposed to change our lives for the better. He ordered a glass of retsina for me and a brandy for himself.

When I told him about my new job he said, 'Good. It's about time you started living high on the hog at someone else's expense.'

I replied stiffly that if he thought I'd risk my career for the sake of a few perks, he had thoroughly underestimated me.

Hugh threw back the remains of his brandy and shook his head. 'What a very naive chap you are,' he said. 'All the best people live at someone else's expense, and always have done. No one in his right mind would rush to become Deputy Marketing Manager of anything unless it involved free travel, a company car, jolly good expenses and probably school fees, clothes, interest-free mortgage and free hairdressing for the wife thrown in for good measure. Not, of course, that you have a wife. Never mind. You can always invent one.'

I told him that obviously all those minor details were being well taken care of. I said, 'You don't honestly think I'd walk into a set-up like this with my eyes shut, do you?' 'Knowing you,' he replied, 'yes.'

Was so rattled by his remarks that I quite forgot to tackle him about the Creative Writing Academy. Left restaurant and ran to post box on off-chance of intercepting collection, but arrived just as van was driving away up the street. Grabbed taxi and told driver to follow van, but lost him in Euston Road. Returned to office by tube, but even so was the best part of thirty bob out of pocket.

Yet another terse note from Ruth about the Barford projections set a miserable seal on what should have been a very happy and satisfying day.

Wednesday, August 16th

Posted *Summer Sonata* to Creative Writing people. I could scarcely bring myself to put the envelope in the box, and as the brown manilla slipped through my fingers, I felt as though part of my soul had gone with it.

Rang Mother this evening for no particular reason. She took an age to answer. When she finally did, I said, 'I hope you're not going deaf; I've been ringing for ages.'

'Not at all,' she replied briskly. 'If you must know, that

dreadful Tony Benn was on TV again and I've been watching with my fingers in my ears.'

Thursday, August 17th

Was clearing my desk before lunch when Hugh rang to ask if I would be interested in his proposing me for American Express Card membership.

Funnily enough, I have been thinking of applying for some time now, largely as a result of those TV commercials I keep seeing. I have never been a great advocate of the 'live now, pay later' way of life, but to be in a position to book theatre seats over the phone, rent a car without leaving a deposit, and earn the respect of head waiters in the best restaurants is no bad thing for a rising executive. Indeed, to be thought uncreditworthy by potential clients would be to undermine the whole purpose of one's existence.

I realize that not everyone is eligible for membership by any means, and I told Hugh that I was most flattered to be asked.

He said, 'There's no need to be. I only mentioned it because they're offering six bottles of rather good wine to anyone who introduces a new member. I'll fill out the form straight away. You're the fourth scalp I've bagged this morning.' And he rang off.

Arrived home this evening to find an application form for membership of the National Trust. £7 a year seems little enough to pay for the privilege of walking into any of the Trust's properties free of charge, and can do me nothing but good in the eyes of my new employers. Have sent off cheque straight away.

Friday, August 18th

Read a fascinating report in the paper about a drugs raid in Chelsea. It seems that the police had been watching the flat for some weeks, but when they finally decided to pounce, they got stuck in the lift between two floors and by the time they'd extricated themselves, the suspects had poured most of their merchandise into the water cistern.

I am rather worried about this, since there is nothing to prevent the stuff getting into the London water system and thence via the taps into our homes. Why they couldn't have shoved it down the loo like every other drug smuggler, I can't think.

One would have thought the authorities would be as concerned as I am, and yet, so far, no warnings have been issued in the papers or on the radio. Really, the public is held in less and less regard these days.

This morning my coffee tasted most peculiar, and I have been feeling decidedly light-headed all day. Mentioned the fact casually to Sarah, our secretary, who said she felt fine and that for as long as she had known me I have been rather airy-fairy.

There's no talking to her since Armitage ditched her for Jane. It's as if the fact that he's gone off with my ex-girl-friend was in some way my responsibility.

Am seriously considering penning a stiff note to the Metropolitan Water Board.

Saturday, August 19th

It never rains but it pours. Have deliberately been maintaining a lowish profile with Amanda during these tricky times, largely to avoid another possibly embarrassing scene with Trubshawe *père*.

Matters taken rudely out of my hands by sudden appearance shortly after breakfast on the doorstep of the young lady in question, carrying a small suitcase, a selection of magazines, and a moth-eaten toy panda.

Any doubts that I might have been harbouring concerning my feelings for her dissolved in an instant, and I opened my arms to her. 'Thank God you're in,' she said, and marched firmly past me into the flat.

'Is anyone else here?' she asked.

I told her that we were quite alone. 'Good,' she said. 'I need your help.'

I said, 'It's right that I should be the first person you turn to at times like this.'

'Actually,' she said, 'you're the third. All the other people I tried were away for the weekend.'

People tend to say things they don't really mean when they're upset. The long and the short of it is that she has had the most almighty row with her parents, given them back her

Mini and left home. I said I hoped I was not the cause of it.

She said, 'Why ever should you think that?'

She then announced that she was planning to move in with me. While I am obviously excited at the prospect of our living together if only temporarily and while I welcome having someone else in the flat to help out with housekeeping, cooking, bills, etc, I certainly do not wish to fall out with Enid and Derrick.

Until this business of expenses, etc. is settled with Barfords, there is always the possibility I may still be working for Derrick for some time to come.

At all events, have decided to play it by ear, at least until after the weekend.

After supper we watched an absurd American detective film on TV, curled up together on the sofa, sipping wine and canoodling.

As I write these words, Amanda is in bed next door with a magazine. The moment of truth is nigh. . . .

Sunday, August 20th

Last night rather a flop – in every sense of the word. Undressed in bathroom, washed carefully all over standing up, and gave teeth a strenuous seeing to – rather too strenuous, as it turned out, since I carelessly knocked the hard part of the brush against my upper gums, drawing blood and slightly loosening a molar. Rinsed as best I could in Listerine and finished toilet with modest dash of after-shave in various strategic places. Arrived in bedroom to find Amanda lying on her back with her eyes closed and magazine face down on her chest.

Thinking to surprise her, I tip-toed across the room. In doing so, small Abyssinian prayer rug beside bed slipped on lino floor, bringing me to the floor with a crash and badly ricking my neck. Amanda did not even stir.

Tip-toed from room again to bathroom where I took two Disprin in water and put on my surgical collar. Realizing I was still naked, I reached behind door for my pyjamas only to remember they were hanging on line over bath, still damp from yesterday morning's wash.

Put on underpants, returned to room and slipped into bed

beside naked, sleeping figure. Despite pain, finally nodded off.

Woken soon afterwards by telephone. Staggered to sitting room to answer. It was Derrick, at his iciest, wanting to know if Amanda was with me. Did the only thing possible in the circumstances by adopting West Indian accent and saying he must have dialled the wrong number. Hurried back to room to find Amanda sitting up anxiously in bed. As I entered, she shrieked with laughter, pointing at me, stuffing the sheet in her mouth and rolling around helplessly. I suppose a surgical collar does look rather funny if you're not used to such things, but not as funny as all that. Against my better judgement, removed offending article and hopped back into bed but sadly unable to respond to her enthusiastic advances. I doubt that even Beddoes would have fared better in the circumstances. Amanda said it really didn't matter and went back to sleep, leaving me to long hours of sleepless agony. Finally dozed off just before seven and managed to get in an hour or two before Amanda appeared with newspapers and breakfast on a tray.

I am not normally one for lying around in bed at weekends, but there are exceptions to every rule. Suffice it to say that one thing led to another and before I knew what, it was lunch-time. I've said it before and I'll say it again, a happy sex life is fundamental to any relationship. Apart from anything else it has also done wonders for my neck.

Monday, August 21st

Rang Hardacre the moment I got in this morning and as tact-fully as possible tackled him over this matter of expenses. He said, 'Of course you get an expense account. How could you possibly do the job otherwise?'

Said that I was just checking on a few details, adding that I presumed that included a company car.

He said, 'Oh, I'm afraid that's quite out of the question. We're cutting back on perks like that.'

Obviously I shall now have to get rid of the VW once and for all and buy myself something more in keeping with my new position. A Rover 3500 perhaps or a Citroën CX. Or even a BMW, though why we should support the German car industry in this country after all the trouble they've given us over the years I cannot imagine. If only Amanda hadn't been so hasty in giving her Mini back to her parents. Much as I am getting used to her presence in the flat, I may seriously have to consider turning her in.

Arrived home this evening to learn that she had spent all day cleaning the flat. To my eye, it seemed slightly dirtier than when I left this morning. Spaghetti for dinner. Her idea of cooking this simple dish is to take a handful of the stuff and force it into the saucepan breaking off all the outside bits which, if they do not fall into the flames of the gas and become welded on to the enamel, scatter in all directions so that the floor becomes like an ice rink.

She also forgot to put salt in the tomato sauce.

I could not be more fond of her if I tried, but really if the last few days are par for the course kitchenwise, I'd do better to revert to the Indian takeaway. On the other hand, no amount of spicy food can make up for a healthy helping of spicy sex!

Tuesday, August 22nd

Had just got in after a longish lunch with Iversen and Attenborough when the chairman's secretary rang to say he would like to see me at 4.15.

I do not think I have experienced a more nerve-racking half hour in my life.

Arrived in Derrick's office to be greeted with the words, 'I hear you're leaving us.'

I replied that in my considered view it was best for all concerned.

'Quite right' he said. 'None of us can afford to turn down good offers nowadays, not with wives and families to support.' Decided to play the innocent and asked him if he happened to know where Amanda was. He said, 'At home, having tea with her mother when I last heard of her. I gather she found all that cooking and housework too much of a strain. Still, plenty of time for all that, eh?'

I said, 'So you know everything?'

He said, 'You mean about her staying with you? Of course.'

I said, 'When? How?'

'Oh,' he said, 'the moment I rang up the other night. That

was quite the worst bit of acting I've come across in a long time.'

Rang Amanda later who said she thought it would be better for both our sakes if we didn't meet for a few days. Had no choice but to agree. Feel I should be putting my foot down over all this, but how? I never thought the day would come when I would value Beddoes' advice. If he hadn't rushed off leaving so many unpaid bills, including his share of the telephone, I might have rung him in Brussels, but not at those prices. Finally decided to do so, reversing the charges.

After a certain amount of to-ing and fro-ing, the operator informed me that Mr Beddoes had refused to accept the call. I can only assume there was some sort of breakdown in communications. What uncertain times we do live in.

Wednesday, August 23rd

Mother's birthday. Hope the flea collar for the cat went down well. Not perhaps the most personal of gifts but, for one who thinks more of her animal than herself, highly suitable, I think. Can she really be 68?

On way to coffee machine this afternoon, spotted Sarah in Iversen's office, obviously collecting money. I wonder what they're thinking of buying me? I could really do with a new wallet. The problem is how to drop a big enough hint without letting on that I've twigged.

Still nothing from Amanda. I miss her dreadfully, but am determined to leave the running to her for once.

Thursday, August 24th

On way into work, stopped off at my local BL dealer to see if they had anything to catch my eye. I feel it is my duty to support the British car industry at this low point in its fortunes. Mr Aylott, a tall, well-spoken young man in a dark suit, sat me down with a cup of coffee and delivered a fascinating lecture on the history and manufacture of the Austin and Morris. He then took me out for a test run in his Rover 3500 and allowed me to experience what he called 'the magic of BL motoring'.

Was particularly impressed by the brakes which are most efficient, if a little sharp – to wit the sharp crack Mr Aylott gave his knee against the dashboard when I stopped suddenly at a pedestrian crossing.

Still, he couldn't have been nicer about it and said he was sure the limp was only temporary and that provided *I* was convinced, it was worth the odd unexpected knock.

We then looked at a selection of second-hand models any of which I'd have been happy to own. Was particularly taken by a white 1976 Austin Maxi. According to Aylott, they are spending £300 on doing it up, including a new clutch, and four hours of paintwork. He says it will look very nice indeed when they've finished with it. I have said I'll think about it. He told me to take my time, pressed some sales leaflets into my hand and limped off towards his office.

Made a point of getting out my wallet in front of Sarah this afternoon and saying it was high time I got a new one.

She said, 'Yes, it certainly is.'

I think the message has got through.

Friday, August 25th

My last day at Harley Preston. In a symbolic gesture, threw my old wallet out of the office window and watched it flutter, like an autumn leaf, into the dustbins below. Then went to wash my hands in gents. Just before five-thirty, strolled into Sarah's cubby hole to find her putting the cover on her typewriter.

'Hallo,' she said, 'you still here then?'

I said, 'If it wasn't for the party, I'd have gone hours ago.'

'Oh,' she said, 'are you having a party? You might have asked me.'

'There seems to be some sort of misunderstanding,' I said.

'Obviously,' she said. 'Well, I must be off.' And she began to gather up her things.

I said, 'About the you-know-what, I couldn't help noticing you were making a collection the other day.'

'Oh, that,' she said. 'It's for Roundtree's secretary, Felicity. She's getting married, you know. As you were leaving, I didn't think you'd be interested.' And with a curt goodbye, she walked off down the corridor.

Was hunting in the dustbins for my old wallet when Armitage walked by.

'What's all this then, Crisp? A last minute spot of industrial espionage?'

I couldn't be bothered to reply.

Saturday, August 26th

My article came back today from the Creative Writing people. Hardly a sentence has escaped the furious attentions of the red pencil, and the margins are filled with lengthy and, to my mind, totally unjustified criticism. *Summer Sonata* was considered 'a sloppy title'. My description of the sights and sounds of Richmond Park in high summer were 'overblown and hackneyed'. As for my unexpected encounter with the young couple making love, this was thought to be 'not credible and rather crude', and my expressions of regret and the loss of innocence 'mawkish and naive'. The comments are signed H.B.-F. It may, or may not, be Hugh – who cares? The point is, a set-up that employs a tutor who is so incapable of recognizing talent when it leaps off the page and hits him in the face is hardly likely to get my vote, and I have written to say so.

Amanda rang this morning to ask me to lunch tomorrow at The Boltons. Have said I'll go, but may easily pull out at the last moment. Later, called round to car showroom to find a stout, middle-aged man with handlebar moustache sitting in Aylott's office. Asked where Aylott was.

He said, 'He's away for a fortnight in hospital, having an operation on his knee. There's a rumour he may never play squash again.' Had been planning to ask for a test drive in one of their Range Rovers, but in the circumstances it seemed only polite to buy the Maxi that caught my eye the other day.

Mr Balditch told me that there were still one or two little things that needed looking at in the workshop.

'We're putting over £350 of work into this car,' he said. 'The paintwork alone will take twelve hours.'

I doubt if one would have met with that quality of service from a foreign car dealer.

Spent rest of day composing two advertisements: one for my Beetle and another for some new flatmates. I obviously cannot rely on Amanda to help out on either score.

I may definitely slide out of this lunch date tomorrow. One

good thing about her departure: at least I can now wear my surgical collar in bed *sans peur et sans reproche*.

Sunday, August 27th

If the Sunday Supplements are not trying to sell off cheap continental quilts and curtain materials, they are trying to foist clock radios and digital watches on to the unsuspecting public. Why anyone should feel the need to be woken up by the inane chatter of Irish disc jockeys first thing in the morning I cannot think. I have woken regularly at 7.30 for the last five years without the need of any artificial alarm, and see no reason to change my habits in the future.

Rang Amanda at noon to say that I had been unexpectedly struck down by a violent attack of food poisoning and would therefore be unable to make lunch.

She said, 'I think it would be to our advantage if you came.'

Arrived in time for drinks. Derrick said cheerfully, 'Something soft for you, I suppose?' And before I could utter a word, he had poured me a glass of Perrier water. Lunch was my favourite: roast leg of lamb, garden peas and new potatoes. Derrick had brought up one of his best clarets.

'Plenty of everything for you?' said Enid and piled up my plate. Amanda came into the room and exclaimed, 'You shouldn't be eating that with your food poisoning,' and took my plate away.

'Just a glass of wine then,' I said.

'Certainly not,' said Derrick.

After a while they relented slightly and allowed me to nibble on a dry biscuit and sip some water. While we, or rather they, were waiting for the pudding, Amanda announced that Derrick had agreed to throw a party for her on September 16th, in return for which she is to undertake a two month's course in shorthand and typing. I'm the last to know – as usual.

We then went through to the sitting room for coffee – or not in my case.

Derrick poured himself a brandy and announced that he had had enough of our shilly-shallying and the sooner we got on with it and made the whole thing official the happier he would be.

In the meantime he has bought Amanda a small house in Parsons Green, if you please. Whether this is intended as a juicy carrot to lure me to the starting gate I do not know. At all events, I was certainly not about to let him think I can be bought that easily.

I said, 'What a very good idea,' and immediately changed the subject to the forthcoming Barford client meeting. By three-thirty was feeling so hungry I made an excuse and hurried home where I ate baked beans on toast followed by cheese and biscuits, two cups of coffee and a Mars bar.

An hour later had one of the worst tummy upsets I have ever known. Still, at least it gave me a much-needed opportunity to lie down and review my situation.

I suppose I am very old-fashioned, but I had always assumed that in the event of my marrying, the role of breadwinner would fall fairly and squarely upon my shoulders. On the other hand, I don't recall the Duke of Marlborough adopting a high moral tone when he married the Vanderbilt girl, and Dickie Mountbatten very quickly adjusted to the idea of marrying an heiress. The alliance of beauty, brains and breeding with money and property is as traditional a part of the English way of life as the Eton Wall Game and Swan Upping. In this life some of us fall on our feet, and some don't, and I must learn to accept my fortune with good grace and press ahead with cheerfulness and humour. I suppose I must now think seriously about putting our relationship on a proper footing and buy Amanda an engagement ring. Now that the problem of accommodation has been settled, I shall be able to spend a little more on it than I had expected.

Monday, August 28th

A ghastly thing happened. I still cannot believe it is true. Woke refreshed and full of optimism after an excellent night's sleep. Looked at my watch to discover it was 9.15! As a result arrived to take up my new appointment three-quarters of an hour late, in a muck sweat and minus my usual bolstering breakfast.

Asked the commissionaire at the front desk for Mr Pratt's office and when lift wouldn't come, ran to the eighth floor, still wearing my motorcycling gear. Flew in through door marked N. G. PRATT, MARKETING MANAGER (NEW

PRODUCT DEVELOPMENT) and came face to face with extremely attractive red-headed girl who said, 'Messengers are on the fifth floor.' I laughed and explained who I was, but she seemed never to have heard of me. At all events, Pratt and Hardacre are both away in Stockholm until next Monday. Hardacre's secretary, Miss Hippo, also away.

The girl told me her name was Pippa Robinson and that she was Pratt's secretary. Suggested she made a few enquiries on my behalf, but she could find no-one who even knew of my presence in the company. I had a mind to kick up a bit of a stink, but did not wish to embarrass Pippa who did her very best to make me feel at home, and made me a cup of coffee on a real Cona machine.

While eating one of her digestive biscuits, I bit hard on the tooth I had loosened with my toothbrush and broke it clean in two. Pippa was most concerned and immediately rang her own dentist and made an appointment for me tomorrow at two-thirty.

I do not think I have ever got on so well with anyone so quickly as I did with her. We seem to laugh at exactly the same things, and there is definitely electricity between us.

At noon, the door opened and a large, shambling man of about forty-five with straggly fair hair round a bald head and strikingly bad teeth stuck his head round the door and said, 'Hallo, who are you?'

I explained who I was, at which he said, 'Good, good. Settling in well, I hope?' and left.

I said to Pippa he looked like a man who had just escaped from a loony bin. She said, 'Actually, that was Harold Hill. He's the chairman.'

Lunched alone at a sandwich bar near the office. One sardine, one cheese and sweet pickle.

At three o'clock a surly looking black woman arrived with the tea trolley. Asked for milk and no sugar and got lemon and three lumps. Later Pippa gave me a Rolo which got stuck in my broken tooth and hurt so much I had to go home. Was almost at the front door when I remembered I was supposed to pick up the Maxi.

Rushed back to the showroom and arrived just before they closed at five-thirty, only to learn that they have had a couple of blokes off sick. Balditch said, 'We do want to bring the vehicle up to standard. After all, we are putting nearly

£400 into it. We should have it ready this time Thursday. No sweat.'

Maybe it wasn't for him, but then he hadn't run half the length of Kensington High Street.

To bed early with the *Evening Standard* and a couple of Veganin. Jane always used to pronounce it as though it were a Russian astronaut. Strange how much I still miss her. She would have been very much my type if it hadn't been for the bad skin. And the hair. The *Standard* has made my sheets quite black.

Tuesday, August 29th

Arrived in Pratt's office, on time, to be told Miss Hippo would like to see me. Confronted by a petite blonde woman in glasses.

She said, 'I'm most terribly sorry about this, but we were expecting you next week. Anyway, I think I've found an office for you. If you wouldn't mind sharing Miss Robinson with Mr Pratt for the time being.' She then led me along the corridor to the back of the building. Couldn't help noticing that she had a pronounced limp, so said conversationally, 'That leg of yours looks nasty.'

'I've got used to it myself,' she said, 'ever since I had polio as a child.'

My office slightly smaller than I had imagined, but it could be worse. It's a pity that in an office block that overlooks such a pretty square I should have a comparatively uninspiring view of the back of the Carshalton Building Society building. Still, I shall probably hardly ever be there.

Hung my calendar from Drake's garage depicting British wildfowl on the wall above my head. Thought of placing photograph of Amanda in black leatherette frame on the desk, but finally decided against it.

I wouldn't want to give the impression unnecessarily that I am spoken for.

After a while, heard the sounds of a trolley being wheeled along the corridor, and cups being chinked. Waited for several minutes but no-one came. Rang Pippa to suggest lunch but no reply. Decided to risk sandwich bar again. Tongue on white with mustard excellent but chicken on brown very nasty indeed.

Bought *Evening Standard* to check on my ad. It certainly stands out very well. I'm glad now I allowed myself to be talked in to the semi-display.

To the dentist at two-thirty. He says I'll need a root filling, followed by a crown.

Although claiming to be National Health, this will set me back £150.

Have said I'll think about it. At that price, it's worth getting some quotes from other dentists. I never thought the day would come when I would have to shop around for a new tooth.

Wednesday, August 30th

Picked six dentists at random from Yellow Pages and they all quote a similar figures, except one in Cricklewood who quoted only £80. Have never been one to spoil the ship for a ha'p'orth of tar, but for £70, it has to be worth the detour and the man sounds really very nice indeed. Have made an appointment for Friday.

After lunch a woman rang to enquire about the car. She seemed very keen indeed and we arranged to meet outside the flat at five-fifteen. Left the office early in order to give the vehicle a quick wash and brush-up prior to inspection. It was a pity a large piece of paint should have chosen today of all days to come away completely, but then it is for good, sound engineering that so many millions have been buying VWs over the past fifty years, not fancy bodywork.

She arrived punctually by taxi, a small, grey woman, not unlike Mother in looks. Name of Miss Timms. The entire transaction took slightly less than fifteen minutes. I was naturally disappointed not to get the £150 I was asking, but I must agree with Miss Timms that 98,000 miles *is* steep, even for a Beetle, and the bodywork *has* seen better days, and the smell inside *is* rather pungent, and although £65 is hardly what I'd call a near offer, I'm frankly quite glad to have the thing off my hands. Whether she really would have reported me to the Trades Description people I don't know, but one cannot afford to take those sort of risks nowadays. Not in my position anyway.

Thursday, August 31st

Called at showroom to collect my new Maxi, but it seems they came across something in the gearbox this afternoon they don't like the look of.

What I'd like to know is, if the car was supposed to be ready by this evening, what were they doing inside the gearbox *this afternoon*?

Did not feel inclined to kick up too much of a stink, however, since they have offered to lend me a two-year-old Mini until Monday evening.

Browsed round a few jewellers' at lunchtime. I had no idea engagement rings were so expensive. Anyway, in my view, if a couple need to resort to flashy jewellery to prove their love for each other it's a pretty poor look-out.

September

Friday, September 1st

To Cricklewood by Mini to see the dentist. I don't know why it had not occurred to me he might be a coloured chap, but it hadn't. However, he appeared to go through very much the same routine as white dentists, so I daresay my misgivings are without foundations.

He seems confident that he can do a good job on my crown for £90, so I have told him the contract is his. We meet again in a week's time.

The only drawback with black dentists is that after staring up into gleaming white mouths for a few minutes one comes away with such an inferiority complex about one's own stained, grey, metal-filled monstrosities. It's a pity *our* ancestors didn't chew a few more roots.

Saturday, September 2nd

It is exactly a year ago to the day that I decided to start my diary. And what a fascinating year it has been. Looking back, I see that in my first entry I remarked that if anyone thought I had undertaken a diary with an eye to publication, they had another think coming. And yet I venture to suggest that my view of the late seventies is every bit as fascinating and revealing and publishable as Harold Nicolson's was of the thirties and forties, if not more so.

I am well aware that the exploits of the rich and famous make for popular publishing, yet Francis Kilvert and Parson

Woodforde scarcely met or wrote about a figure of note in their lives and today their diaries are considered classics.

Sunday, September 3rd

Woke to discover that I have developed some sort of infection in my broken tooth. Rang dentist, but no reply. Like plumbers, they are never there when you want them. Patched up tooth as best I could with oil of cloves and took a healthy dose of Codein, which I have repeated at three-hourly intervals. As a result, left later than expected to collect Amanda for Tim and Vanessa Pedalows' cocktail party.

Had not in fact realized they were back together again, and can only hope Vanessa has forgiven me for my seemingly treacherous behaviour re Tim and the German air hostess. Hared along Earls Court Road and was waiting innocently at traffic lights by tube station when a young man in a Morris Minor drew up next to me, wound down his window and called out, 'Afternoon, Fittipaldi. You were hammering it a bit back there, weren't you?' If there's one thing I can't abide it's self-righteous busybodies, and I decided to cut him down to size straight away.

'I think that's a matter for a policeman to decide, don't you?' I replied.

He got out of his car, came across and waving an identity card under my nose, said, 'I am a policeman. May I see your driving license, insurance and MOT certificate?' I tried to explain that it was not my car, but this only made matters worse. Whether he thought I'd stolen it, I don't know, but before I knew what, we were both standing at the side of the road while he took down particulars. He explained that he would have to report the incident and that I might be hearing more about the matter or I might not. He also insisted on a complete examination of all my tyres, including the spare. As a result arrived at The Boltons three-quarters of an hour late, with filthy hands, only to receive an even greater shock, if such a thing were possible. Amanda has gone punk. Vivid green- and orange-striped hair sticking up like a gollywog, funny signs painted all over her face, skin-tight pink satin trousers, tee-shirt knotted at the hip, the lot. She took one look at my filthy hands and said, 'Great. Wipe them all over me.'

There's only one way to deal with people who set out deliberately to shock one's sensibilities and that is to pretend one has not even noticed.

Everyone at the Pedalows' so taken by her appearance that no apology or explanation was needed. Philippe de Grande-Hauteville, who is still convinced I work for the BBC, put on a typically Gallic performance, kissing his fingers into the air in an exaggerated fashion. I had no idea that he and Theresa Milne had married. Obviously they've wasted no time in producing a family: Theresa was looking like the side of a house.

'When's the baby due?' I asked her.

'I had it two months ago,' she said, and walked away. Oh dear, oh dear.

Bryant-Fenn came bouncing up, gave me a friendly slap on the face and said, 'You're a dark horse and no mistake.' He would have to choose the side of my bad tooth. Announced he had just been appointed Wig and Hairpiece Editor of *Barbershop Quarterly*, and thought he might do a feature on punk wigs, and could he use Amanda as the model?

Tempted to bring up subject of Creative Writing Course and show him up for the shallow poseur he really is, but honestly he is so obviously second-rate, one can't help feeling sorry for the fellow.

'My dear chap,' I cried. 'Feel free.'

He gave me a sickly grin and rolled off into the crowd. Had been studiously avoiding Vanessa but need not have bothered.

'How's my favourite traitor?' she shrieked, rushing up to me and patting me enthusiastically on my bad cheek.

Mentioned my unfortunate brush with the law to Tim who said, 'Oh, that's nothing to worry about. Take my advice and write a nice cringing letter to the Chief Traffic Officer saying what a naughty boy you've been and you'll never hear another word about it. I do it all the time. Never fails.'

He and Vanessa have asked us to Covent Garden on Tuesday for a gala evening of ballet. Had in fact been planning on watching the first episode of the much-heralded TV series about the Prince Regent that night. However, when Tim explained that not only would we be guests in their box, but that we were invited to the glittering party afterwards, I decided Prinnie could do without me for one week. After all, what is TV glamour compared with the real thing? There's no knowing who one might not meet at that sort of do. Amanda, to my surprise, has said she'd love to come too. Not looking like that, she won't.

On the way out from the party, felt a tap on the shoulder and whirled round only to receive a sharp blow on the side of the face from a man who said cheerfully, 'Sorry, old boy. Thought you were someone else.' No need to say which side of the face.

Spent the rest of the day swilling down Codein and hot tea. I don't know which is more painful: my toothache, or the prospect of walking into the Crush Bar at Covent Garden with a green-haired zombie on my arm.

Monday, September 4th

Rang Amanda first thing to re-state my views concerning tomorrow night, only to be told by Enid that she had already left for the secretarial college. I had completely forgotten she was starting there today. I said, 'If she gets bored she can always staple her ear lobes.' Enid claimed not to know what I was talking about, but I think she got the point.

She has suggested an outing to the theatre on Saturday evening – just the two of us. I am not sure how to interpret this. Asked what play she had in mind.

'You're the expert,' she said, 'I leave it entirely to you.' If she's not hatching something I'll eat my hat.

Had my first meeting with Neville Pratt and Keith Hardacre. It could not have gone better. My first task is to prepare a proposal document for a major presentation of Brand X, as the new product is now known, in a fortnight's time in New York! Am so excited at the prospect of my first visit to the New World, I can think of nothing else. Not only that, but I am also to work in close co-operation with Roundtree and Ruth Macmichael at Harley Preston. I cannot wait to see their faces when I confront them for the first time as the client. There'll be a few old scores settled now and no mistake.

Arrived back from lunch to find a man painting my name on the office door. Pointed out that it was Simon, not Stephen. He has said he has another job on today but will do something about it as soon as possible.

Tooth still extremely painful, despite Codein. I am up to ten a day now.

Collected car after work. It seems to go very well, apart from the slight stammering in top gear. Rang Balditch when I got home. He says it is probably just the new clutch settling in. I wasn't even aware it had a new clutch.

Tuesday, September 5th

So nervous at thought of how Amanda will go down with this evening's balletomanes that I was scarcely able to concentrate on anything else all day.

Left office early, bathed, dressed and drove to Boltons to collect her. Stomach full of butterflies. Could hardly believe my eyes when she walked down the front stairs in a most elegant black evening dress, blonde hair done up in elaborate creation with ribbons and wild flowers. I suppose it must be a wig. I have never seen her looking lovelier, and said so.

Set off in excellent time for the Garden. No sign of Pedalows, so stood by bar with Amanda viewing audience. Shocked to see how few men had followed my example by dressing. One or two were actually wearing jeans and open-necked shirts. I'm surprised they were allowed in.

Just as the first bell was sounding, in swanned Tim and Vanessa, cool as cucumbers, asking if I'd collected the tickets. Had been looking forward to a leisurely pre-performance whisky and soda, but instead had to battle in long queue at box office. Was making my way across to the others when who should I bump into but Armitage and Jane? He in one of his cheap, off-the-peg three-piece monstrosities, she in a particularly frumpy peasanty number. Most unsuitable.

'Evening, Crisp,' said Armitage loudly. 'Fancy seeing you here. We're in the stalls; where are you?'

I told him Box 69.

'Bad luck,' he said, and the pair of them walked away. I put it down to envy.

Naturally had imagined that at £11 a head we would be prominently placed in first tier and the fact we had to climb several sets of stairs did not bode well. Arrived finally at box. I have never been higher up in a theatre. Since there was room for only three chairs at the front, I had to stand at the back from where I could barely see half the stage. Not surprisingly, much of the first item lost on me – literally.

During first interval, spotted a chap I once met at a dinner party, named Cyril Bunting. I smiled at him but he did not smile back. Such a crowd, I was quite unable to get near enough to bar to order drinks before bell went.

Had assumed that after the interval Tim would suggest taking turns with the standing, but he said nothing and resumed his seat. Item two starred the famous Russian dancer Baryshnikov. From the few glimpses I caught of him as he flashed on and off the small portion of the stage that was visible to me, he certainly seemed a very lively young fellow.

In second interval, I was all for going straight to bar, but Tim announced we should change seats.

We eventually found some in the stalls which we took just as the lights were dimming. I was sorry the man in front of me had quite such a large head; however, by crouching slightly and bending to my right, I had an almost uninterrupted view.

To the Lyceum Ballroom, of all the unlikely venues, for the exclusive gala party. Rather too exclusive as it turned out, since Amanda's and my name not included on invitation. As a result had to battle in undignified fashion with three sets of bouncers before being admitted.

Sat near the door in order to spot the famous as they arrived. Tim and Vanessa pointed out several including, I think, Princess Margaret. It was a pity they didn't actually know any of them to speak to.

Later, several elderly people took to the dance floor in an abandoned sort of way. Amanda was all for joining in, but I put my foot down. Or rather, I didn't!

Ordered coffee which did not come and left at 11.45. So much for the all-night revelry I had been anticipating. Still, an instructive evening, though I was sorry to have missed Prince Regent. With TV you really feel you get to know the famous.

Wednesday, September 6th

It's an extraordinary thing, but the more Codein I take, the worse my toothache seems to get. Am now up to two every two hours. Rang the dentist but he cannot see me till Friday.

Amanda rang after lunch to say that Timmy and Joanna

had suggested we all go on Thursday to the opening of a new discotheque called the Top Hole. A typically suggestive name, I thought, but she couldn't see it. When I asked her why she wasn't at college she said she was so tired after last night she had decided to take the day off. I said, 'You'll be even tireder after tomorrow night.'

'Oh do stop fussing,' she said. 'Anyway, dancing's like rugger. The spectators are always more tired after a match than the players.'

I should have thought the sum total of her knowledge of rugger could be jotted down on the back of a postage stamp. However, have agreed to make an exception to my night-club rule for no other reason than that it might take my mind off my toothache.

Have also bought two tickets for *Once in a Lifetime* at the Aldwych. I have heard excellent reports of it. At £5.30 a ticket, it ought to be good.

Thursday, September 7th

Our soirée at the Top Hole as dismal and depressing an affair as I had feared and expected.

Place so full of freaks and grotesques that Amanda looked positively square in her punk gear. Oddly enough, my dark suit and OF tie came in for much favourable comment. Spotted several faces that were vaguely familiar from the newspaper. Also had quite an interesting chat at the bar about the weather with a girl who might or might not have been Britt Ekland. Timmy and Joanna shared several cigarettes during the course of the evening.

'Pot?' I enquired casually.

'No,' said Joanna. 'Poverty.'

I laughed. It was a good try but I'm too old a hand to have the wool pulled over my eyes.

Tooth started playing up later, so took a couple more Codein.

'Uppers or downers?' Joanna asked me.

'Neither,' I replied coldly. 'Codein. For toothache.'

Timmy said, 'You don't want to take too many of those; before you know what, you'll be hooked.' A marvellous joke suddenly occurred to me. 'Talk about the *pot* calling the kettle black,' I said, but of course the joke went way above their heads. I am beginning to wonder if the younger generation have any sense of humour at all.

Dancing on the whole abysmal compared with the days when I pulled off Twist competition in Obergurgl.

I don't know what got into me but on a whim I grabbed Amanda's arm and before I knew what, I was in the middle of the floor, shaking my hips and waving my arms like a mad thing. Was in the middle of one of my famous shoulder shaking routines when I distinctly heard a girl's voice behind me say, 'It's pathetic to see these middle-aged people making fools of themselves.' At this everyone within earshot, including Amanda, burst into gales of laughter. I left the dance floor at once – probably forever.

In the car going home Amanda announced that the theme of her party on Saturday week is to be punk; anyone who comes dressed in any style other than punk will not be admitted. Oh dear. Trouble.

Friday, September 8th

To the dentist at long last. Mr Nwachukw most concerned about the pain in my tooth, and when I told him how many Codein I was taking he tutted in a most worried way. Having never been in a position to stretch a dentist's skill beyond a straightforward filling, I was rather pleased at being able to present him with a problem he could really get his teeth into. (No joke intended there.)

After a long, muttered conversation with his female assistant, also black but rather attractive in an African sort of way, he turned to me and announced he would have to give me a general anaesthetic and 'have a bit of a look-see'. Luckily, it was some hours since I had last eaten, and I agreed to his suggestion without any hesitation.

While under the gas I had the most extraordinary erotic dream concerning Mr Nwachukw's assistant. Came round to find the pair of them roaring with laughter. I said, 'May I be allowed in on the joke?' at which they roared all the harder until the tears ran down their cheeks. I grinned foolishly, until Nwachukw announced that he had just removed the whole tooth.

I was astounded and reminded him that he had referred to inspection rather than extraction.

He said he was very sorry, but that under the circumstances he had no alternative, and once again the two of them shrieked with laughter. I pointed out stiffly that the pain was, if anything, worse.

Nwachukw told me, that was because I'd become too reliant on pain-killers. The more one takes, the worse the pain.

I laughed and said, 'You make me sound like a junkie.'

He said, 'You are.'

I do not suppose that he meant it literally. On the other hand, I must admit that I was beginning to look forward to my next Codein with something approaching pleasure, and it is a great relief to know that I shall now have no further need of them and can kick the habit forthwith.

Got back to office and went straight to gents where I gave myself a long, hard look in the mirror. Suddenly noticed that the area below my eyes has gone quite dark, and it was then that the horrible truth dawned on me: I was staring at the face of a potential drug addict. It just goes to show how easily the most respectable of us can unwittingly find ourselves caught up in the sordid net of depravity.

Am so relieved to have escaped that I am seriously thinking of joining one of these drug prevention organizations and using my experience to help others like me. Meanwhile I must prepare myself for the long period of cold turkey that inevitably lies ahead.

With my tooth still extremely painful, the going is going to be tough, but I think I can take it.

Saturday, September 9th

Woken early by Enid ringing to say that some friends had just arrived unexpectedly from America and would I mind terribly if we called off our theatre visit this evening?

Didn't say so, but in fact quite relieved.

Remembering our last evening à deux, back in May, and the emotional landslide that resulted, I feel that any attempt on either of our parts to stir up old embers would be bound to end in tears. I know there are young men who think it clever and amusing to carry on with a mother and her daughter at the same time, but, attracted as I am to both of them, I do not hold with it, and that's all there is to it.

Popped round to the Aldwych to return my tickets, only to

find a long queue in the foyer. From what I could make out they all seemed to be trying for *Once in a Lifetime*, and apparently without success.

Young man behind the grille most unhelpful and told me that under no circumstances could they refund money on tickets. I said that I would be perfectly prepared to change them for another evening, but that was out of the question too.

Decided to take my revenge by selling my tickets to one of the people in the long queue behind, only to find that for some mysterious reason not one of them wanted to see *Once in a Lifetime*.

I can't say I blame them.

It's at moments like these one really misses *The Times* letters column.

Sunday, September 10th

Gum very sore but am resisting Codein bravely.

Car still stammering in top gear, so decided to ginger up the system by driving down to Kent for lunch with Mother. Rang Amanda at eleven to ask if she'd like to come, but informed by Enid she was still fast asleep. Exhausted from a hard week's typing and shorthand, I suppose. When I told Enid of my plan for the day she said, 'We were expecting you for lunch to meet our American friends.' I thought she sounded rather disappointed, but reminded her that I am not the only one given to changing his mind at the last moment.

Enjoyed my drive to Kent, despite heavy traffic in Bexleyheath, which for some reason I always muddle with Bexhill. Perfect September weather so that we were able to sit in the garden with our sherry.

Mother unable to resist a series of side swipes at Tony Benn who has evidently ousted Mr Callaghan as her personal Enemy Number One.

'You know all these people at the BBC,' she said. 'Can't you get yourself onto "Any Questions" and really give him a piece of your mind?'

I said, 'Actually, I really do believe he's one of the most sincere men in British politics.'

'So was Hitler,' she replied.

'Hitler wasn't in British politics,' I said.

'Why must you always split hairs?' she said.

I don't know why I allow myself to get drawn into these absurd arguments. I blame Nigel and Priscilla myself. If they had not taken it into their heads to give her that dreadful Burmese cat for Christmas, she might have retained some vestige of sanity. I suppose I should be grateful that *she* hasn't yet taken to creeping up behind one's deck chair and sinking her teeth into one's calf for absolutely no reason.

I never thought the day would come when the sight of Denys Ramsden bumbling through the French windows would actually prove a welcome relief.

Am more convinced than ever that those two are having an affair. At one point actually caught him holding Mother's hand under the table. It's only a matter of time before I surprise the pair of them rolling round on the sofa.

After coffee Denys said he had to be getting home. He kissed Mother goodbye, stepped into his Triumph Mayflower and reversed smartly into my Maxi, completely destroying the rear offside door. In the circumstances he seemed extraordinarily unabashed. It's more than I can say for my car.

As I was leaving, Mother remarked, completely out of the blue, that she thought dentists had given up gas years ago. I felt like saying it's a pity someone doesn't give Denys Ramsden a few sniffs to settle him down.

Monday, September 11th

My third day off the drugs. A remarkable achievement considering pain in calf caused by cat's teeth. Still, it helps draw attention away from my tooth. Should I be considering an anti-tetanus shot, I ask myself.

Rang my doctor re use of gas by dentists and he confirms Mother's assertion. Am beginning to wonder if I have not unwittingly become involved in some seedy racket or other. I dread to think what happened while I was under the anaesthetic. Any day now I'll receive a lewd photograph of myself and the receptionist plus a demand for a large sum of money, I shouldn't wonder. The extraction of the tooth was probably only a cover. If so, it was in pretty poor taste.

Ruth Macmichael rang just before lunch to suggest a meeting about Product X. She sounded unusually respectful, as well she might be from now on. It's a pity I cannot say the same for the Personnel Department at Barfords. Despite constant requests, I still have no secretary of my own. Must also insist on someone coming and re-doing the sign on my door; I can't really believe they *still* haven't heard of me in Office Services.

In the meantime, have penned a stiff note to Miss Hippo concerning the continuing non-appearance of the tea trolley at my end of the corridor.

New York presentation plans coming along very well. My idea for incorporating clips from Woody Allen films in the audio-visual section makes all the difference.

After work, took car to garage. Mr Aylott still away with his knee, but Balditch says they have a spare door in the work-shop and I should be able to collect it on Friday. They will also look into stammering.

Tuesday, September 12th

I think I may have succeeded in kicking the drugs once and for all. Pain in mouth and ankle barely noticeable. I can only hope now that my neck doesn't go. That would throw me on to the horns of a dilemma.

To Harley Preston in the afternoon for a meeting with Ruth about Product X.

It was a curious feeling to walk through the familiar front doors knowing that if it weren't for people like me they wouldn't be in business at all.

Announced myself to Lorraine, the pretty but bad-tempered-looking receptionist. She put down her emery board with a sigh and said, 'Was it business or pleasure?'

I wasn't going to take that sort of talk from anyone and said severely, 'I'd be glad if you'd tell Miss Macmichael I'm here.'

'What was your name again?' she said.

I pointed out that she might not be aware of the fact but I had worked there for three years until very recently.

'No,' she said, 'I'm not.'

I said with cold deliberation, 'The name is Crisp. Barfords.'

'Suits you,' she said.

I replied, 'And you'll be finding out how much in due course,' and left the building and returned to the office.

A drastic step, some may say, but I'm an old enough hand

at this game to know that it never pays to fool about with the client, and it won't do Harley Preston any harm to sweat on the top line for a bit.

Waited in my office all afternoon for a panic-stricken call from Ruth, but not a peep out of anyone. Phone finally went at six-fifteen. It was Bryant-Fenn to say he had been ringing me at home for the last half hour to invite me to a party he is giving on Friday week at some hotel near Guildford.

He said, 'I'm surprised a man in your position can get by without a telephone answering machine. I certainly wouldn't be where I am today without mine.' Wherever that might be!

He's right though. From now on, more and more people *will* be wanting to get in touch with me at odd hours of the day and night. I might seriously consider looking into the possibilities.

Wednesday, September 13th

A glorious, sunny morning, yet tinged with a sense of sadness. Arrived in the office in a strange mood. Even stranger when I found there was still no message from Ruth. Spent morning ringing round answering services. Have plumped for one in Wimbledon.

After lunch, rang Ruth and said casually that I was sorry not to have made our meeting yesterday.

She said, 'It wasn't yesterday, it's today. In half an hour.' Flew round in a taxi. Receptionist, who obviously still had no idea who I was, told me to go straight up to Ruth's office.

I said, 'Are you sure she didn't mean the board room?'

'Quite sure,' she said.

Ruth perfectly friendly, although I think she might have been a little more apologetic about Roundtree's absence. I should have thought in the circumstances he could have arranged to see his chiropodist another day.

I said, 'What? No tea then?' in a half-joking way.

She said, 'This is a business meeting', and proceeded to discuss the New York sales presentation. I do not believe I have ever been spoken to so insultingly in all my adult life. She was particularly scathing about the inclusion of the Woody Allen clips in the audio-visual section. I tried to explain that *of course* they were old hat, that was the whole point, and that they made a perfect satirical counterpoint to the projected sales figures.

She said, 'Crap. That's the trouble with this country. Jokes, jokes, jokes. That's the only thing anyone can make any more. And not very good ones at that. Well, in New York, we're pretty goddam serious about business and we leave the funnies to TV, and the sooner you understand that, the better.'

I said stiffly, 'You seem to forget, Miss Macmichael, that Product X is *our* product and the way we choose to present it to the public is our affair. You are simply here to advise us, not to teach us our job. I call the shots round here now.'

She folded the papers up into a file, handed them to me across the desk and said, 'You may be the client now, but you're still as big an ass-hole as ever. If you don't take my advice, we're none of us going to be calling any shots from now on.'

I have not as yet decided what steps to take in this sorry matter, but steps there must be.

A more immediate worry, however, is Amanda's party on Saturday. If it is to be a punk affair, as she says, I really do not think I can invite any of my friends. Except perhaps Bryant-Fenn. He'd go to a chimpanzee's tea party if it were free.

This evening a polite young Indian wearing a large ring came and demonstrated the answering machine. Japanese, of course. However, it seems to fit the bill very well. £175 a year, to be precise. It should be delivered in about a month. I can't wait.

Thursday, September 14th

At a meeting in Hardacre's office to discuss New York, Pratt said, 'Ruth is right. The Woody Allen stuff must go. The charts need clarifying, too.'

When you can't rely on your own people to back you, who can you rely on? He's obviously terrified of Ruth. On the way out, Miss Hippo handed me my passport with my American visa. It is for four years, so obviously someone is thinking long term.

Worked on charts and audio-visual till lunch, then rang Bryant-Fenn about Saturday. He accepted, needless to say. Walked up to Oxford Street in the sunshine and bought myself a box of safety pins, a lavatory chain and some pink washable hair dye.

Friday, September 15th

Spent morning putting final touches to audio-visual. Just before lunch called in at Miss Hippo's office to collect my air ticket. Rather disappointed to note that I am booked on a 747, despite request to 'UPGRADE TO IST CLASS IF AVAILABLE.' I chaffed her and said, 'I thought all top executives these days flew by Concorde.'

She replied, '*Top* executives, yes.'

I said, 'Just as long as I don't suffer too much from jet-lag.'

She replied, 'It shows how often you've flown the Atlantic. That only happens on the way back.'

I said, 'Not necessarily,' and left it at that.

As I was going to lunch, I suddenly realized there had been no mention of a money advance from Accounts. Have rung my bank and ordered dollars and travellers cheques for first thing Monday morning.

To garage on way home to collect car, but apparently they didn't have a new door in stock after all. I told Balditch to keep the car and have it ready by the time I get back from New York. He was obviously impressed.

Saturday, September 16th

Rang Amanda first thing to ask if there was anything I could do to help with the festivities. A man's voice replied, 'I doubt it. This is the robing room of the West London Magistrate's Court.'

Thank heaven I didn't announce my name. I have no wish to prejudice my case when it comes up. *If* it comes up. The worst part of being a criminal is the waiting.

Took the phone off the hook so as not to be disturbed and spent the morning running over my commentary to accompany the projected sales figures.

After lunch, dyed hair. Had hoped to achieve a slightly patchy effect, but while lowering right side of head into mixture, my foot slipped and I plunged my whole head in, eyebrows and all. The effect was so sensational could not resist looking at it each time I passed a mirror. By tea-time had become quite used to the colour – though not, I must say, to the curious smell.

Later, had a couple of large whisky and sodas and attempted to insert a safety pin in right cheek. According to Amanda there is a way of doing it whereby you suck in your cheek thus making the skin very thin. Can only assume she left out some vital instruction since I was quite unable to insert the point without great pain and a certain amount of blood. No amount of love is worth a nasty dose of gangrene. In the end, settled for a neat compromise by sticking a pin to each cheek with strong glue and attaching a lavatory chain to right ear lobe by ditto means.

Dressed in oldest jeans, ski-ing anorak and a pair of pointed boots I have been meaning to throw out for years. At 8.30 rang for a minicab only to realize my phone had been off the hook all day.

Arrived at Boltons in fine fettle. Door already wide open and sounds of revelry issuing into warm night air. Marched through hall and sitting room and issued into marquee in garden with a gay shout of 'Ta ra!' Everyone stopped talking and turned to stare at me. I could not believe my eyes. They were all dressed in conventional evening frocks and dinner jackets. There was a moment of complete silence and then the place erupted into laughter.

Amanda came up to me, looking enchanting in a long white billowing number. 'Oh dear,' she said, 'I've been trying to ring you all day, but your phone's been out of order. We decided at the last moment to change the theme of the party from punk to Deb's Delight. I assumed you'd come in a d.j. anyway.' Took the only course open to me and left the room with calm dignity. Rushed upstairs to guest bathroom, filled the wash basin with warm water and lowered head into it. Shampooed hair five times, but to no avail. Finally slipped down back stairs, out through side door and into street. Glimpsed two figures in intimate conversation by lighted sitting-room window. They looked very like Amanda and Bryant-Fenn to me. They're welcome to each other. I have more pressing things to worry about – chiefly how to get this wretched dye out of my hair before leaving for New York.

Before going to bed, penned a formal note to Bryant-Fenn saying I should not be able to make his party on Friday since I should be in America. Thank goodness.

Sunday, September 17th

Up at seven thirty after a wretched night's sleep to start hair washing. At noon was on my thirteenth wash when the phone rang. Rushed to answer it, hair still dripping wet. It was Amanda to ask where I had got to last night; she had been worried.

'Obviously not worried enough to tear yourself away from Bryant-Fenn's side,' I said briskly. At this she burst into tears, moaning that what should have been the happiest night of her life had turned into the most miserable. She should talk!

Put the phone down only to find that, all the time I had been talking, my hair had been dripping on to the carpet, leaving a large pink stain. It never rains but it pours these days. (A grimly apposite metaphor in the circumstances.)

Afternoon divided equally between washing hair and carpet, though without obvious success on either score. I may have to resort to some sort of hat, though quite what style I cannot think. In fact I don't seem to be able to think constructively about anything any more. I hope I haven't got water on the brain. That's all I need.

Monday, September 18th

Up early and out to the shops to buy a hat. Finally settled for a shapeless tweed affair that folds up into a little bag specially for travelling. It makes me look a bit like Rex Harrison. I cannot think why I have not treated myself to one before, pink hair or no pink hair.

Hurried home to breakfast and pack. Suddenly remembered I had still to collect my foreign currency and travellers' cheques. Flew to bank in taxi. Not only was the stuff not ready, but I was forced to waste further valuable time signing every single cheque in the presence of the cashier. He said, 'If I were you, I'd apply for an American Express card.'

Arrived at check-in desk for the New York flight to discover that the flight had been delayed for an hour.

Asked girl about possibility of being up-graded to first class. She punched several keys on her computer, and said, 'We are expecting one other first-class passenger. If he doesn't show, you're in.'

Asked if in the meantime I could wait in VIP lounge.

'Don't push your luck,' she said.

As we were boarding I was accosted by name by one of the hostesses and shown to a seat in the first-class section. Wasted no time taking off my shoes, slipping into lightweight airline slippers and stretching out luxuriously. The film, I noticed, was *Capricorn One*. I always enjoy a good thriller and have been cursing myself for missing this particular one in London. Was trying on sleeping mask when the hostess arrived to say she was very sorry but the extra passenger had turned up after all and would I mind moving back into the tourist-class section.

Nearly all seats by now taken, so forced to squash in amongst a group of chattering Chinese slap underneath the cinema screen. Not that it mattered since the tourist-class film was *Players*.

After lunch, settled down to make some last-minute changes to audio-visual script, but almost at once the entire Chinese contingent decided to fall asleep and snored so loudly I was quite unable to hear myself think.

In the end compelled to stick in earphones and watch film. I liked it no better the second time.

Despite hat wedged firmly on head, Customs man at Kennedy immensely rude about my hair and made me turn out entire contents of my suitcase. As I was doing it up, one of the buckles came away in my hand.

'That's the trouble with imitation leather,' he said.

Car ride into city so terrifying that the famous Manhattan skyline almost entirely lost on me.

The hotel seems reasonably comfortable and well appointed, if a little far from the centre of things. 8th Avenue and 22nd Street is not exactly Cole Porter country. I quite agree with the bellboy that it is convenient for Greenwich Village – not that that is a great advantage to me since the Kellerman Corporation is in East 59th Street. Still, I gather taxis are easy enough to come by, even in this part of town.

Have been here less than an hour as I write these words, and yet already I can sense the excitement of this great city coursing through my veins like young wine. Am feeling decidedly light-headed. But then, of course, I am on the 28th floor.

Tuesday, September 19th

Harry Colouris rang first thing to say some important people had just flown in from Philadelphia and did I mind very much if we put off the rehearsal till this afternoon. Couldn't have been more delighted.

8th and 22nd not in fact the easiest place to find cabs, but finally struck lucky and took material to Kellerman's offices on East 59th. Thought I'd spend rest of morning sightseeing. Called at nearest bank to change some travellers' cheques. The clerk peered at the cheques for a long time, then said he was very sorry but he had never heard of the Bank of Scotland and had I any means of proving their bona fides. Asked to speak to his superior who said he'd heard of the Bank of England, but the Bank of Scotland was a new one on him. He said if I'd had American Express travellers' cheques, why, he'd have been happy to oblige, and his colleague said, 'Don't you have American Express cards in England?'

I said, 'It depends who recommends you,' and left it at that.

Tried several more banks with similar results. Finally tracked down a bureau de change in the Rockefeller Centre and changed £10. In my view anyone who walks round New York with large sums of cash in his pocket is asking for trouble.

Made first for Empire State Building. Am a firm believer in the E. M. Forster philosophy that the best way to get to know a new place is just to walk about aimlessly, and would certainly have gone there on foot, but one hears all too many stories of visitors being mugged in broad daylight.

Cab driver most friendly and talkative. Was sorry I couldn't place the exact street in Wembley where his brother-in-law has his take-away Chinese, but assured him I knew the general area pretty well.

As I was paying him, he said, 'Normally I won't have a faggot in my cab, but I made an exception, seeing as you're British.'

Made a mental note to speak sharply to the girl who sold me the hair dye.

View from Empire State Building all it's cracked up to be, if a little hazy. Unfortunately, effect rather spoilt by the fact that I was suddenly seized by an overwhelming desire to throw myself off the top. In spite of high fencing all round had to hold myself against back wall and will myself not to rush forward and start clambering over the wire. It is moments like this that lead one to ponder how many other strange, irrational urges lie deep within our subconscious.

To lunch at Ma Belle's on 45th Street, as recommended by Keith. They have old-fashioned telephones on the tables and you can make free calls all over New York. If you know anyone to ring, that is.

Was in the middle of my hamburger when suddenly the phone on my table rang. Picked it up and received an obscene message. It was obviously a wrong number, so replaced the receiver and asked waitress for a portion of apple pie and cream. Two minutes later, phone rang again. Message of even more pornographic nature. Decided enough was enough. Told the waitress to hold the apple pie and cream, and went to pay my bill. As I was leaving, I noticed a couple of young men, obviously pansies, looking at me, and giggling like a couple of school girls. I ignored them. I've no idea what it was all about, but am quickly coming to the conclusion that New York is a city even more obsessed with sex than London.

Discovered I now did not have enough money for a cab, so ran to Rockefeller Center where I changed £20. As a result arrived slightly late at Kellerman's. Even so, rehearsal could not have gone better, and I think we are all set for tomorrow. Afterwards Harry said, 'You know what would have really made that audio-visual? A little touch of humour. A couple of clips from a Woody Allen movie – something like that. They love to laugh, those guys from Cincinnati.'

A very embarrassing thing happened after dinner. Felt I should repay my host's hospitality by taking them all for a drink to the Rainbow Room. When the bill came, found I had not got enough money. Luckily they couldn't have been nicer about it. Decided to come clean and explained my theory about muggers.

Harry said, 'You're kidding. Give a mugger a hundred bucks, he'll take it and run. But a mugger finds you got no bread, he'll be so mad he'll beat hell out of you.'

As we were leaving, one of the guys said, 'Simon, one word of advice. Next time you come to New York, get yourself an American Express card.'

Wednesday, September 20th

I think someone was trying to break into my room last night. I called out, 'I've got a gun in here,' and whoever it was went away. Breakfast took an age to arrive. When it finally did, I said to the waiter by way of a joke, 'Oh, that surely can't be for me. I only ordered mine an hour ago.'

'You're right,' he said, and wheeled it away again.

Had meant to do some shopping in Fifth Avenue on way to presentation, but by the time I had been to the Rockefeller Center to change some more travellers' cheques, there was no time.

Do not wish to tempt providence by commenting on success or otherwise of presentation at this stage, but I don't believe an important man like Arthur Kellerman would have bothered to come up to me afterwards and congratulate me if he didn't mean it. Cincinnati team also most complimentary and expressed particular interest in the technical side of the presentation.

One said, 'I only have one criticism. There weren't too many laughs.'

It is most gratifying to know that my first instincts about American business methods have been proved correct after all. Perhaps I should seriously consider emigrating to America. Work-wise, New York seems to be shouting 'Yes' to me at every turn.

On the way out, Harry suggested that by way of celebration I might like to check out the famous New York night spot, Studio 54. Returned to hotel and was slipping room key into door when a couple of men came up behind me and seized me by the arms. One never really knows how one is going to behave in an emergency until it occurs, and I was interested to notice how calm I was.

I said, 'Now look here, I'm English.'

One of the men said, 'So?'

Could see I was unlikely to make headway on moral or touristic grounds, so immediately changed tack.

'I've got quite a lot of money on me, if that's what you're thinking,' I said.

'That some kind of bribe?' the other man asked.

I said, 'It's an odd way of putting it, but I suppose you could say so.'

The first man said, 'All righty. Let's see what we have here. Attempted bribery of a police officer, threatening behaviour, possible possession of a firearm without a licence. You know where that puts you? Down the tubes, baby.'

Of course, it was only a matter of time before everyone realized it was all a complete misunderstanding. Unfortunately, it meant I had to cancel my sight-seeing trip on the Circle Line boat. Still, it's not everyone who gets to experience the inner workings of Manhattan South police headquarters at first hand.

Dined with Harry at Sardi's which was a great thrill. Looked around in the hope of catching sight of some of the big Broadway stars waiting for the first editions, but as Harry pointed out, nine o'clock is a little on the early side. Took a cab to 54th Street and joined the crowds milling about outside Studio 54, all dressed in the most outlandish clothes and trying to catch the doorman's eye. Was on the point of suggesting to Harry that we called it a day when the doorman shouted out, 'The weirdo over there with the pink hair and the Ivy League boyfriend.'

Harry said, 'That's us. Let's go,' and before I could stop him he had hustled me through the envious hopefuls and in through the doors. While Studio 54 has done nothing to change my attitude towards discotheques in general, I am not so narrowminded that I am incapable of recognizing a life enhancing experience when I have one.

I'm afraid I had to draw the line at accepting invitations to dance with men, but I had a most interesting talk with a very odd-looking fellow with glasses and white hair, and danced quite a lot with a very tall girl who said she was some sort of actress. It was difficult to hear above the din but I thought she said her name was Ernest Hemingway. Could that be possible? Altogether a most stimulating and instructive evening.

The song writer got it right: New York, New York *is* a wonderful town.

My only worry is that I seem to have gone slightly deaf in one ear.

Thursday, September 21st

Had originally planned to stay till Friday, but Harry has had to fly to Chicago and, much as I'd have liked to stay on, I really cannot afford the time.

Arrived at Kennedy in good time for flight. Delighted to discover that the film in tourist class was *Capricorn One*. Found myself a seat with a good view of the screen and no one on either side of me. Was congratulating myself on my good luck when one of the hostesses leaned across and informed me that, since the flight was fairly empty, they would be very happy to upgrade me to first-class. No second invitation was needed. What I did not know until I had taken my seat was that the film in first-class was *Players*. However, thanks to airline's abundant hospitality with wine bottle, I slept soundly most of the way to London and missed it completely.

Woke, bleary-eyed and with a slight headache to learn that the film of *Players* had broken down after fifteen minutes and they had shown *Capricorn One* instead.

Arrived home to find that my American Express card had been delivered during my absence, plus a newsletter and the offer of six King Arthur plates, commissioned specially for Card Members by the International Arthurian Society. Funnily enough the Camelot legend has always interested me.

Unpacked, washed, made tea and rang Amanda.

My heart leapt with joy to hear her voice again.

'Oh,' she said, 'I wasn't expecting you.'

'I came home unexpectedly,' I said.

I suppose in the circumstances I should not be surprised or disappointed that she has arranged to attend a pop concert at Wembley with Timmy and Joanna, but I am.

On second thoughts, though, it's probably just as well, since I am feeling decidedly disorientated. Ah well, that's jet-lag for you.

Early bed with an apple and *People* magazine.

Friday, September 22nd

As soon as I got into the office, rang Bryant-Fenn to say that, since I had come home earlier than anticipated, I should now be able to accept his invitation for this evening.

'Oh,' he said, 'that's very awkward. The fact is, I've just agreed the final numbers with the hotel and frankly I'm not sure I can change them again.'

Not surprisingly, I was pretty shocked at being spoken to like that by an old friend; however, I was certainly not about to let him think I cared two hoots whether I went or not.

'I quite understand, Hugh,' I said quietly, 'There's no need to explain further.'

'I would say come along anyway and take pot luck,' he went on, 'but the thing is, the hotel is laying on individual dishes.

'Tell you what, I'll give them a quick bell and see if they can squeeze you in. No promises, mind. I'll call you straight back.' And he rang off.

Waited for an hour by the phone but no reply. Decided I had wasted enough time over this trivial matter and strolled along to Pratt's office to give him a preliminary briefing on the New York presentation. He said he was very pleased at the way it had gone. Damned civil of him, I must say. Bumped into Miss Hippo in corridor on way back to my office.

She said, 'I heard your phone ringing and took the liberty of answering it. Someone called Hugh.'

'Did he leave a message?' I asked.

'Yes,' she said. 'He said to tell you it was no go.'

'I see,' I said. 'He didn't by any chance say anything about popping in for a drink after dinner or anything?'

'No,' she said.

Looking through *Evening Standard*, discovered *Capricorn One* was showing at my local Odeon. Could not believe my luck. Rang Amanda to suggest going, but the maid told me she had gone to the country and would be back tomorrow. Rang Miss Hippo re my office door. She says a man is coming next week.

Took myself off to the cinema after supper only to learn that *Capricorn One* had come off yesterday evening.

I asked what was showing in its place.

'*Players*,' said the girl.

Saturday, September 23rd

An awful lot of nonsense is talked about jet-lag, but until one has experienced it at first hand one has no idea of how strangely it can affect one.

In my case, it seems to take the form of an overwhelming desire to retire to bed. I do not know if other jet-setters react in the same way, but I almost feel like writing to the *British Medical Journal* to suggest a full-scale survey into the effects of this most baffling condition.

Slept solidly till noon. Indeed I think I could have slept all day had Vanessa Pedalow not rung to ask why I was not at Hugh's 'thrash' last night. I was in no mood to pull punches.

'Because,' I told her, 'I was informed that my unexpected presence would upset catering arrangements.'

'I can't think why,' she said. 'The place was swarming with all sorts of strange people.'

I said, 'I understood from Hugh that the dishes were cooked individually. What did he give you? Half a lobster each?'

'Good Lord, no,' she said cheerfully. 'Hungarian goulash. There was plenty to go round. Tim had three helpings, Amanda had two and so did I and there was plenty left over at the end.'

This was the first I had heard of Amanda being invited, and when I asked Vanessa if she was sure Amanda was there, she replied, 'Yes, of course. So was her mother. What a nice woman and so good looking for her age.'

All very suspicious I must say.

To the garage after lunch to collect my car. The new door looks very good, and stammering completely disappeared. Is it my imagination or is the clutch much stiffer than I remember?

Sunday, September 24th

An astounding turn of events.

Denys Ramsden is dead.

Mother rang first thing with the news. It appears that while sitting on the loo, he pulled the chain and brought the whole cistern down on his head, killing himself instantaneously. Naturally I said I'd drive down to Kent straight away. The maddening thing was, I had been looking forward to a good lie-in to counteract this wretched jet-lag. Everything seems to happen to me.

Was just leaving when Amanda rang and began a long rambling explanation about Hugh's party. However, when

I told her the news she stopped short and said that she would very much like to come too. Drove straight round to Boltons and picked her up. As soon as I saw her, dressed in black, all my old feelings for her came flooding back, fresher and stronger than ever. For two pins I'd have taken her back to the flat and made passionate love to her there and then. Strange how the oddest emotions take over at the most unsuitable moments. But then, of course, in the midst of death we are in life.

It was nearly the other way round when halfway down the M2, she suddenly announced that on more than one occasion Bryant-Fenn had proposed an affair not only to her but also to Enid. Could have made a scene there and then, but decided, under the guise of family grief, to play the matter very cool indeed and made no comment.

Arrived at Mother's to find her in sparkling form, so much so, that I could not help feeling we had been brought there on a fool's errand.

'It was your idea to come,' Mother said.

I reminded her how upset she had been on the telephone.

'Oh that,' she said. 'I blame the cat myself. Staying out all night like that. I hardly slept a wink for worrying. Anyway, panic over.'

I could not believe my ears and asked her if she had any feelings for Denys whatever.

'I daresay I shall miss him,' she said. 'But really it's difficult to feel a lot of sympathy for a man who is so lazy he can't even be bothered to stand up to flush the loo.'

Amanda very subdued all day, I noticed. She couldn't do enough to help Mother. I think the message has got through.

On the way back to London I said to Amanda: 'That wig is really excellent.'

'What wig?' she said.

I said, 'That blonde wig you're wearing to cover up your green hair.'

She said, 'The green one was a wig, this is my own.'

Clutch so stiff by the time I got back to London, I could hardly move it.

Monday, September 25th

For the first time since I arrived at Barfords, the tea lady deigned to make the detour to my office with her trolley. Her name is Agnes, she wears a knitted woollen hat and shapeless slippers several sizes too large, and exudes all the charmlessness and glowering resentment that we have come to expect from our cousins from the West Indies.

'Aha,' I cried as she loomed large and menacing in the doorway, 'so you have found your way at last to the condemned cell.'

'Coffee?' she said, 'or tea?'

I asked her jokingly if there was any difference.

'I haven't got all day, dearie,' she said.

Really what is the point in trying to make these people feel at home? I honestly believe it would be easier to get a laugh out of a Martian. And yet whenever I come across a crowd of black people together, they are invariably dancing about, shrieking their heads off and slapping their thighs. What on earth do they find to laugh at? Us, I suppose.

To Parson's Green after work to view Amanda's little house. It seems pleasant enough, as late Victorian villas go, though hardly what I'd call a desirable residence, or a particularly up and coming area. Still, she seems very tickled with it, and I hadn't the heart to say what I really thought.

There is a fair amount of building work to be done and the inevitable skip is already parked outside the front door.

Amanda rushed up and down showing me which walls would be coming down, where the RSJs would be going and how the gas-fired central heating boiler will fit in the space under the stairs. To my surprise, she has already furnished one bedroom in a haphazard sort of way, and there is a sofa and a coffee table in the sitting-room.

Her enthusiasm is so infectious and she was obviously trying so hard to make me feel at home that when she suggested I stayed to supper, I fell in with the plan as eagerly as I later fell into her rather small bed. Despite cramped conditions, was immensely cheered to realize once again, despite our intellectual and mental differences, we are physically completely in accord. So much for Bryant-Fenn's little challenge.

Have taken car back to garage and Balditch has promised to have it ready by tomorrow evening.

Tuesday, September 26th

To the office in heady mood. All my worries of the last few days seem to have fallen from my shoulders like an old overcoat. The truth of the matter is that far too much of my time is devoted to taking on other people's moral and emotional burdens when I should be putting my own house in order. Why should I give a hoot because a pip-squeak like Bryant-Fenn fancies my fiancée? If our love is not strong enough to withstand the fumbling advances of a frustrated outsider then last night was nothing more than an empty charade.

Rang Ruth at Harley Preston to report on presentation. She responded with grudging praise. Could not resist putting her in her place by mentioning the Americans' comments about lack of humour.

'That figures,' she said. 'Those guys in Cincinnati always were a bunch of ass-holes.'

Amanda rang later to suggest a cinema followed by supper in Parson's Green, but I told her I had far too much work to clear up following my New York trip. Although she didn't say so, I think she was hoping to persuade me to move in with her. All in good time!

Collected car. Clutch fine and vehicle now going perfectly. I see symbolism here.

Wednesday September 27th

A ghastly thing has happened. A pop group has moved in upstairs.

Woken shortly before one by a loud twanging of guitars being tuned. Had just nodded off again when the group struck up in earnest, practically blasting me from my bed, so great was the volume of sound they made.

I stuffed some cotton wool in my ears and lay there in a fury while my bedroom reverberated with their harsh chords and heavy percussion.

Finally made up my mind to go up and say something when the sound stopped as abruptly as it had begun. I can only hope that last night was a flash in the pan, otherwise I can see I'm going to have to take steps.

Thursday, September 28th

One of the worst night's sleep I have ever had to endure in my life thanks to the extravagant musical cavortings of my new neighbours.

When, by three o'clock, the noise still showed no signs of abating, I seriously considered going up there and giving them a piece of my mind. On the other hand, one has to watch one's step with those sort of people. They're almost certainly on drugs and there's no knowing how they might react. Also, one always feels at such a disadvantage in pyjamas.

Compromised eventually by banging on ceiling with the handle of the squeegee, but merely succeeded in dislodging a large piece of plaster which came down on my bedside table, upsetting a glass of water over my pillow.

I'll give them one more chance and that's it.

Friday, September 29th

That's it. Noise last night worse than ever. Walked into the kitchen this morning to discover that a rather charming art deco meat plate that I keep propped on a shelf above the draining board had fallen on to the floor, bringing a salt and pepper mill with it. Miraculously nothing was broken. What amazes me is that no one else in the block has said anything. Still, the sort of people I have as neighbours are so feeble that if someone was being murdered in the corridor they'd claim it was nothing to do with them. Well, I'm very sorry but I'm afraid I have more sense of social responsibility than that, and if young people do not understand how to behave properly in society, then it's up to others like me to put them in their place.

Rang the Managing Agents as soon as I got in this morning and they have promised to look into the matter. In the meantime, I must do something about these bags under my eyes.

The more I think about it, the more ridiculous it is of me to strike moral attitudes where my sleeping arrangements are concerned.

Popped home after work to collect a few bits and pieces. Just to be on the safe side, took down the meat plate. Unfortunately the stupid thing took it into its head to slip out of my hand, bringing down several pieces of china, every one of which smashed to pieces on the floor. Something tells me it is high time I moved out of here.

Saturday, September 30th

My current run of bad luck continues apace. Woke early after a surprisingly good night's sleep in Parson's Green and thought I'd surprise Amanda with breakfast in bed. Slipped into my trousers and zipped up my weasel in my flies. I do not know how this happened. It is certainly not something I have ever come across before. All I know is that it proved to be one of the most painful experiences I have ever known. To add to my humiliation, the zip became inextricably jammed. Luckily, Amanda remembered that the workmen had left a pair of pliers in the kitchen but not before I had undergone several minutes of the most excruciating agony. I'm sorry I couldn't join Amanda in seeing the funny side of it, but there it is.

It may not be a serious enough case for out-patients, but we can certainly say goodbye to 'Sportsnight with Coleman' (Amanda's term for our love-making, not mine) for quite some time to come.

Stayed up after Amanda had gone to bed to watch the first in this new series of chat shows. Everyone seemed to enjoy themselves very much – and so they should with the fees they are paid, but frankly it didn't impress me. I would not have minded so much if the show had been live, but the knowledge that I was being kept up late and having my time wasted by people who were already home and in bed made the whole affair doubly irritating.

October

Sunday, October 1st

The start of the pheasant shooting season (or it would be if it were any day other than Sunday) and for me the beginning of autumn proper. My favourite season. I realize it's fashionable nowadays to pooh-pooh Keats, but he certainly got it right as far as this time of the year is concerned: it really is the season of mists and mellow fruitfulness. And yet, despite a golden walk in Richmond Park with Amanda, felt enormously depressed for most of the day. Autumn, like sex, is strangely bitter-sweet.

Monday, October 2nd

Woken at Holland Park by the postman bringing a recorded delivery letter from the West London Magistrates Court summonsing me to appear on Thursday, November 9th at 10 a.m., to answer my speeding charge. Apparently I may simply plead guilty by letter and have the case disposed of in my absence. I can imagine that a lot of people, fearful of publicity and of further damaging their case, would gladly take that way out, but I have no intention of doing anything of the sort. I am not afraid to stand up in open court and plead my case and, if it should get into the papers, I think I can handle the consequences. Justice, I believe, should not only be done but seen to be done, and you can't *see* anything by letter.

Tuesday, October 3rd

There was a time when I used to look forward to the cheery sound of the morning post plopping on to the mat. Not any more. This morning, for instance, I receive a letter from the landlords stating that they intend to put my rent up to some preposterous amount. Shall have no hesitation in taking my case to the rent tribunal. We'll see what they have to say about it. Weasel still extremely sore. I knew I was wrong to have used that Elastoplast.

Wednesday, October 4th

The thing one misses most during this *Times* strike is the obituary column. Not that I am expecting my own death to be recorded for a while yet but, as Denys Ramsden remarked only a week or two ago, 'Who wants to die in the *Telegraph*?'

In the event, his own worst fears were unhappily realized.

Thursday, October 5th

A most extraordinary thing happened tonight in the Bordelino. While I was finishing my soup, Mollie Marsh-Gibbon lit a cigarette. We were in the middle of a most interesting discussion about *À la Recherche du Temps Perdu* when a small man with a shock of grey hair got up from the next table, came across and asked in a slight Irish accent, if Mollie would put out her cigarette since it was offensive to other diners.

She said that as a matter of fact she did mind, whereupon the man said, 'What do you think about this then?' and spat in my soup. Luckily I had very nearly finished, so it didn't really matter, and we were able to laugh the matter off. Even so . . . are there no lengths these Irish fanatics will not go to to achieve their selfish ends?

Friday, October 6th

Priscilla has rung to ask us both down to Hertfordshire for the weekend on the pretext of watching James competing in his first gymkhana and have accepted. A weekend away will do us both good. Assuming my weasel picks up, that is.

Today marks the end of my sixth week at Barfords and yet the Deputy Marketing Manager is still, as far as any casual visitor to his office is concerned, is a man called Stephen Crisp. Somebody is going to be treated to one of my famous tongue sandwiches on Monday morning.

Saturday, October 7th

A beautiful sunny morning. Just the day for getting out of London. It's a pity we didn't do so earlier and thus miss the Saturday morning traffic jams all the way out to the M11.

By the time we arrived at the farm just after one, the sky had clouded over and it had started to rain. Not only that, but there was a note on the door in my sister's handwriting suggesting that we should meet them at somewhere called Archer's Field near Chelmsford for a picnic. She had drawn a rough map showing us how to get there – a little too rough, as it turned out, since we became completely lost and it was nearly two-thirty when we finally drew up amid the horse boxes.

Parked near the main ring and tracked down the Joyces huddled under the tail-gate of their Range Rover, drinking coffee from a thermos. Nearby was James in a velvet hat and jodhpurs, perched on a short fat grey pony. At our approach, he jumped up and down with excitement, shouting 'We've got the best picnic of everyone in the whole place. Chicken legs and ham and hard-boiled eggs and sausages and Coca Cola.'

I said cheerfully, 'That sounds marvellous, we're starved.'

Priscilla said, 'That's a pity. We've just this minute given your portions away to the Finch children.'

Nigel added, 'Barbara Finch doesn't seem to have a clue about catering.' I felt like saying that his wife was not exactly brilliant in that department either.

Amanda said, 'Actually, I'm not hungry at all,' which obviously endeared her to Priscilla, and from that moment on the two of them got on like a house on fire.

Nigel leered at Amanda for a while, then turned to me and said, 'She rather reminds me of that last girl you brought down. What was her name?' Considering the way he and Victoria had behaved on that occasion I am surprised he should have the gall even to mention the subject.

'I can't remember,' I said. 'She meant nothing to me.'

Strolled across to give James's pony, Misty, a closer look. Was just admiring its withers when the animal suddenly took it into its head to deposit a large load all over my suede shoes. Everyone seemed to think it a great joke. As I was scraping the stuff off, I tried to make light of the incident by saying that it made a nice change from the dog dirt in London.

Priscilla said, 'Ugh, how disgusting – straight after lunch,' and James declared in a loud voice that he felt sick. In my opinion it wouldn't do him any harm to *feel* something useful for a change, like the business side of his father's hand across his backside.

Wandered across to the collecting ring where James's class was gathering in preparation for the Bosanquet Cup.

Came upon two small boys feeding a fat brown pony with slices of ham and hard-boiled eggs. I asked them if by any chance they were the Finch boys, 'Yes' they said.

Re-joined the family group in time for James's round. Nigel and Priscilla obviously deeply embarrassed when Misty refused every jump he came to, and when James whacked him with his stick, he deliberately walked through every one, flattening them all to the ground.

I called out, 'Come in, number eighteen, your time is up.' One or two people laughed, but Nigel went white in the face and hissed, 'You can keep your London witticisms to yourself, thank you very much.' If there's one thing worse than competitive parents, it's parents who cannot take a joke at their children's expense.

Arrived back at the farm at last at six-thirty, cold and hungry. Attempted to warm myself up with a hot bath and a whisky and soda, but stomach so empty that I merely succeeded in making myself rather tight. Matters not helped by Priscilla insisting on my sleeping in the same spare room to which I was banished when I visited last year with Victoria. It was, if anything, even colder. Consequently shivered my way through supper for which we were joined by an unsmiling young man with a mass of curly hair and a ring through one ear named Andrew.

I gathered he is an agricultural student, not that that entitles him in my book to sit down at table with filthy finger nails. His manner predictably dour and charmless. Attempted to draw him into the conversation by raising various subjects of rural interest including the Common Agricultural Policy, farm subsidies, the rights and wrongs of blood sports, foot and mouth disease and so on, but I might as well have been talking to a turnip.

To bed at ten with a hot water bottle and a slightly sore throat. Harbinger, no doubt, of a nasty cold. That's what you get for leaving London. For all their jeering at urban civilization, country people are forever going down with some minor ailment or other, and is it any wonder?

Sunday, October 8th

This is positively the last time I bring a young woman to stay under this roof. A year ago almost to the day, Nigel seduced Victoria, and last night I am convinced that some sort of hanky-panky went on between Amanda and Andrew. I admit my evidence is purely circumstantial, but I'm not a fool. Girls do not develop small bruises on the sides of their necks overnight for no reason, nor do they suddenly start exuding the odour of the farmyard unless they have recently come into very close contact with it indeed. Amanda's explanation that Andrew had suddenly offered to show her the new pig unit simply will not wash. At twelve thirty at night?

Would have raised it with her had there not been more urgent matters to attend to, namely helping Priscilla to canvass on behalf of their Conservative candidate, Ivor Hitchens, who is standing in the local by-election. Had supposed there would be more to it than walking down the street banging on people's doors, announcing that Mr Hitchens was in the neighbourhood and asking if they'd like to meet him. On the other hand, it is given to few of us in these days of TV electioneering to experience an election at grass roots level, to test the nation's pulse for oneself and dip one's toe in the water of public opinion. Most encouraged to discover that not one of the householders in Church Lane, Back Street and Stortford Road who answered our knock expressed anything other than pleasure at the prospect of an exchange of views with our candidate.

Indeed, we very soon found we had left him far behind.

'He's doing far too much talking,' Priscilla muttered angrily as she strode past us. So as a result were we.

'I'm not sure if we're on the register,' one man told us.

I said, 'Well, why not talk to Mr Hitchens anyway?'

The man replied, 'I don't mind talking to him, but not to you.'

I thought it was rather uncalled for. Still, in the hurly-burly of the hustings one has to learn to take these little knocks in one's stride. All in all, a fascinating afternoon. How reassuring it is to know that in this great country of ours, each and every one of us has a small but, I believe, not insignificant role to play in the shaping of our destiny.

Throat slightly better, but car slightly worse, for no obvious reason.

Monday, October 9th

Arrived at office to find a note from Harold Hill asking me to come and see him at the earliest opportunity. Having had no dealings thus far with the chairman, I was not sure how to interpret this. Obviously it had something to do with my American trip, but what exactly? Showed note to Pippa and asked what it meant. She looked at it carefully and said, 'It means he wants you to go up and see him at the earliest opportunity.'

In the event he could not have been more friendly and invited Amanda and me to his house at Maidenhead for the day on Saturday. Of course I accepted at once. 'Good egg,' he said. As I was leaving I remarked casually, 'I rather thought this might have something to do with the New York trip.'

'What New York trip?' he said.

Rang office manager to say that if something is not done about the name on my office door by the end of the week, there's going to be trouble. 'Oh yes,' he said. 'Who are you again?' I sometimes wonder if I work here at all.

Tuesday, October 10th

I have never thought of myself as a political animal, yet I do not believe I have ever been quite so excited by anything as I was by this morning's edition of 'Yesterday in Parliament' on Radio 4.

Only those who have campaigned at grass roots level can really appreciate the cut and thrust of parliamentary argument, and I am seriously beginning to wonder if my own talent for debate is not woefully wasted in the commercial world.

If so, I realize only too well the importance of having the right woman at my side. Churchill certainly would not have got where he did without his faithful Clemmie, nor Harold Macmillan without Lady Dorothy. Whether I can depend on Amanda Trubshawe for similar support is becoming an increasing cause for doubt in my mind.

Pippa, on the other hand, would make an ideal statesman's wife.

Wednesday, October 11th

Once again my instinct has been proved correct, to wit the letter I received this morning from the chairman of the local branch of the Conservative Association in Essex thanking me for my efforts at the weekend and adding that my keen interest in the future and well-being of the Conservative Party has been noted at the highest possible level. No prizes for guessing who that refers to, and a personal message from the No. 10 direction cannot be ruled out by any means.

Thursday, October 12th

Tim Pedalow rang this morning to invite me to a wine tasting on November 8th. I have enjoyed drinking wine for many years and it has long been a source of regret to me that I am not more of a connoisseur. This may be just the opportunity I need to start educating my palate. Have told Tim that I cannot be certain of my plans so far ahead, but *en principe* would be happy to accept.

While I was out at lunch, someone changed the name on my door from Stephen Crisp to Stanley Crisp.

Friday, October 13th

One's first priority in politics is a sense of responsibility towards one's constituents, and the fact that I alone of all the tenants in the block was prepared to take the lead in putting a stop once and for all to the nocturnal cavortings of this pop group proves that I am made of the right stuff.

The fact that there turns out to be no pop group living in

the flat upstairs, only a tiny, grey-haired lady with insomnia is, as I pointed out to Amanda, neither here nor there. The fact that I was prepared to assume the responsibility is what matters. After all, I might just as easily have been confronted by a drug-crazed lunatic with a knife.

'What I can't stand about politicians,' Amanda said, 'is that they are always poking their noses into other people's business.'

I said, 'So you don't see yourself as the chatelaine of Chequers?'

'No,' she said.

Am definitely going to ask Pippa out for a drink next week.

Saturday, October 14th

To lunch with the chairman at his house at Maidenhead. It only goes to prove what a great mistake it is to have pre-conceived ideas. I am not saying I do not like Scandinavian, open-style architecture, or housing estates, or home-made wine, or fish fingers, or children under the age of five, or even devoting most of Saturday afternoon to washing Ford Cortina 1.5 Ghias; it's just that I had expected something different.

Harold (as I now call him) could not have been more welcoming. It was a pity, as he said, that they should have been out of gin *and* whisky, but I am really quite fond of straight Noilly Prat, and one drink before lunch is really quite enough for anyone.

Betty Hill is really not as bad a cook as she likes to make out. Anyone can forget to put the lamb chops in the casserole until ten minutes before one is due to eat, and I do see, when you have three small children, it can so easily slip one's mind to take them out of the deep freeze first. (The chops, that is, not the children!) On the other hand, the rice pudding was excellent, if a little hard, and perfectly complemented the stewed plums.

We had a most interesting talk over lunch, mainly about Greece where I gather Harold and Betty take a villa every summer – or did until the children came along – and I was most fascinated to learn that the large marble in the bottom of my rather small wine glass is an old Corfiot custom, used originally to ward off evil spirits.

Harold obviously much taken by Amanda. Wish I could say the same for his wife.

As we were leaving, impulsively seized fifteen-month-old Daniel, swung him with a cheerful cry high into the air, and cracked his skull smartly on the main beam. Why the Scandinavians have to build their ceilings so low I cannot imagine. Perhaps they never lift children above shoulder height indoors.

However, the doctor assured us there is no question of a fracture. Did not like to ask about chances of permanent brain damage, preferring to keep that little worry to myself for the next few years. Finally got away at about six.

One of the windscreen wipers fell off on the M4.

Sunday, October 15th

One can scarcely pick up a newspaper these days without coming across a reference to this self-improvement course that everyone is talking about.

I am the first to admit that I am far from perfect and I would certainly be interested in the possibility of tuning myself up morally and mentally. £195 seems little enough to pay for the secret of a happy life, but not if it involves spending a whole weekend at some draughty country house with a lot of people I don't know, feeling their faces, making public confessions about my sex life, and rolling round on the floor screaming my head off. The truth of the matter is that we all spend far too much time worrying about ourselves and not enough worrying about other people.

The more I think about it, the more convinced I am that I am naturally cut out for politics.

Perhaps I should make a start by taking up social work in my spare time?

Monday, October 16th

On an impulse, rang poor old Miss Weedon's bell last night on my way in from the office and asked her if there were any little chores that I could help out with.

Knowing how sensitive the elderly and impoverished can be to the merest hint of charity, I approached the matter with immense tact.

'If ever you need any little jobs done,' I told her, 'like shopping, for instance, please don't hesitate to ask.'

'Thank you,' she replied, 'but that won't be necessary. Harrods' delivery service has always proved more than satisfactory.'

Tuesday, October 17th

My weasel now completely recovered from being zipped up, though the way things have been going with Amanda since the unfortunate affair with the baby on Sunday, this is of small consolation.

To add to my problems, I find I have now contracted athlete's foot – a cruel irony, since I rarely indulge in any physical activity of any kind, on the athletics track or off. Perhaps I should. The phrase *mens sana*, etc. did not acquire popular coinage in ancient Rome for nothing.

Wednesday, October 18th

By an odd coincidence, amongst my mail this morning what should I find but a leaflet advertising a local Yoga group. Read the whole thing with the keenest interest. While the essence of Yoga is the discovery of oneself through meditation, there are many other benefits to be derived from the 12-week course, including better breathing, relaxation, weight loss, mind control and goodness knows what else. Am particularly interested in the Yoga philosophy. The first class takes place next Thursday and I have rung up already to enrol Who knows, they may be able to do something for my athlete's foot!

Thursday, October 19th

Was returning to the office in a taxi, following a working lunch at Thomas de Quincey with Gubbins, the head of our Manchester operation, when Pratt suddenly announced that if I didn't do something about Pippa very soon, he'd go round the bend. When I asked him what he meant, he replied that for the whole of this week she had been saying she must see me.

'Obviously,' said Pratt, 'she's got the hots for you, old

chap. If I were you, I'd get in there while the going's good. There's a formidable list of contenders waiting to take your place.'

If this is true, and I see no reason why Pratt should be trying to deceive me, then it is without doubt the most astonishing stroke of luck ever to come my way.

Tempted to ring her at once and fix a drink or dinner, but a) it never pays to look eager, and b) I have committed myself to a number of projects with Amanda over the next few days which I cannot possibly get out of. Nor do I wish to.

Athlete's foot showing no signs of improvement. Have been using the cream in conjunction with the powder, as per the instructions, but am beginning to wonder if these are not meant to be applied separately. If the manufacturers mean that, why on earth don't they say so? One does not need to be a professional to recognize bad marketing when one sees it.

Friday, October 20th

To the Phoenix to see the Stoppard at last with Amanda and the Pedalows.

An extraordinary thing happened during the second act when the man sitting in the row in front of us suddenly threw back his head and started uttering curious gargling noises from the back of his throat.

Tim who was sitting in an aisle seat said, 'I don't like the sound of this. I'm going to ring for an ambulance.' And leaping to his feet he hurried towards the back of the auditorium. Although the man continued to utter these horrible sounds, no one apart from us seemed the slightest bit concerned, least of all the woman seated next to him who was presumably his wife.

I turned to Vanessa to ask what she thought we should do but at that moment a man in the row behind us leaned forward and hissed in my ear, 'Quick, grab his tongue before he swallows it.'

I said, 'Are you sure?'

'Of course I'm sure,' the man replied. 'I am a dentist.'

Pushing past Vanessa, I bent over the poor fellow and shoving my hand into his open mouth, seized his tongue with my two front fingers. Suddenly the man opened his eyes and sat upright. Naturally I at once let go of his tongue.

'Who are you?' he asked in a loud voice. 'And what do you think you're playing at?'

Attempted to explain how this curious state of affairs had arisen, but he was not to be appeased.

He said, 'Things have come to a pretty pass when a man can't doze off in a West End theatre any more without inviting bodily abuse from fellow members of the audience.'

A classic case of much ado about nothing, some might say. On the other hand, if he really had been suffering a heart attack and one had pretended not to notice, one would almost certainly have been accused of gross callousness. One simply cannot win these days.

Saturday, October 21st

To the Horses of San Marco Exhibition at the Royal Academy, and not before time, since it comes off in a week. Whether the horse they had brought over from Venice was the one that Carlo Mendotti so signally failed to show me when I was in La Serenissima in May with Hugh, I have no means of telling. If so, I am sadder than ever not to have seen this magnificent work of art *sur place* in St Mark's instead of on a carpeted platform being gawped at by swarms of culture vultures who have probably never been within a thousand miles of Venice in their lives.

Afterwards, in Piccadilly, bumped into Harold and Betty Hill, up for an afternoon's shopping with the children. They seemed friendly, if detached. I was sorry that little Daniel had to scream quite so loudly when I bent down to tickle his chin. He looked sweet under his white bandage. Jason and Emma, however, could not have been more friendly and jumped up and down, pulling on my coat sleeves and generally getting over-excited. Quite why Jason had to hit me in the groin like that I can't think. I suppose he was trying to attract my attention. If so, he certainly succeeded. I admit I must have cut a rather curious figure, doubled up and groaning all over the pavement, but if Harold had only had the sense not to laugh out loud, his beastly little brat would not have assumed he was being given the go-ahead to hit me again in exactly the same place.

Is it any surprise I have decided to give Parsons Green a miss this weekend?

Sunday, October 22nd

Lunch *chez* Trubshawe. The first time in many weeks. No matter how much I protest otherwise, they are convinced I am living with – and by implication, off – their daughter.

It's a pity she does not share my eagerness to disillusion them, but I suppose that's her way of showing her independence. However, Enid has invited me on to the committee of the local branch of the Conservative Association. Have said that my new job leaves me little time for extra-curricular activities, but that I'll certainly think it over very seriously.

Mother rang this evening to tell me to watch 'Face the Music' as Lord Norwich was on. The way I'm feeling I could not have cared less if the entire House of Lords was appearing. Which reminds me, I never heard another word from Hardacre about the National Trust.

Monday, October 23rd

Rang Pippa as soon as I got in this morning and invited her to the National on Wednesday night to see the Maugham.

She sounded most surprised and said, 'Oh, really, it's not necessary to go to such lengths.'

Not wishing to take too much for granted, I said, 'What sort of lengths did you have in mind then?'

She said, 'A quick drink after work. That's all it'll take.'

Pratt was obviously right after all. I don't know whether I am more excited or alarmed. I know we are only going to the theatre, but I feel I am committing adultery already.

Tuesday, October 24th

Delayed ringing Enid while I sorted out my thoughts. The way things are going with Pippa, there seems every possibility my relationship with Amanda may soon be at an end and I would not wish to embarrass her mother by having to face her across the committee table. On the other hand, sentimentality has no place in politics, and any work on behalf of the Conservatives can do me nothing but good.

Rang her after lunch to deliver my verdict.

'Oh,' she said, 'it never occurred to me for a moment that you would refuse.'

From what I can gather, she is expecting me to get up a committee of my own to devise some sort of fund-raising event to take place early in January. When I asked her what she had in mind, she said, 'I've no idea. That's up to you.'

While I welcome the responsibility, I shudder at the deadline. But then, of course, some people are good organizers and some aren't.

Wednesday, October 25th

So nervous at the prospect of this evening I could think of nothing else all day.

Need not have worried, as it turned out, since Pippa is the easiest of companions and most amenable to every suggestion – unlike some I could mention.

What a pleasure it is to spend an evening with someone who share's one's own tastes so exactly. Noticed in the second act that one of the actors was wearing an OF tie. Must remember to look him up in the OF register – if and when the secretary decides to send me the new one.

Supper at the Bordelino devoted entirely to the subject of Harold Hill. Pippa seemed to know all about my visit to Maidenhead and wanted to hear everything about it down to the last detail. Tempted to redirect conversation into more fruitful areas, but left the restaurant sadly unprepared for any possible advance in our friendship. Supposed she would suggest my stopping off at her flat for coffee, and was naturally disappointed when she got out of the car, thanked me for a most pleasant evening, and without so much as a backward glance, disappeared inside her front door.

Now what have I done wrong?

Thursday, October 26th

Pippa polite and cheerful as ever in the office but no mention of last night. Have always prided myself on not acting the Beddoes or the Armitage as far as women are concerned. However, feel I could certainly take a leaf out of both their books over this one.

Arrived in good time for my first Yoga class. Why is it

these sort of activities always appeal to the most unattractive people? The slight hint of self-improvement and out they come, the beards, the sandals and the dirndl skirts. But then, I suppose, those sort of people are more in need of self-improvement than most.

We all trooped into the school gymnasium (unheated, of course) where our teacher, a thin woman with a monotonous voice named Mrs Hodges, taught us how to sit in the lotus position – that is to say, cross-legged on the floor, with our backs straight, our wrists resting lightly on our knees and our thumbs and middle fingers forming a figure O. She then told us about the need for proper breathing, through the nose and the mouth. As one who has been using this method for many years with considerable success, I found no difficulty with this. One or two of my fellow students, however, seemed to be making unneccessarily heavy weather of this simple device – so much so that one was tempted to ask them how they'd been breathing hitherto: through their ears?

If nothing else, evening classes are great levellers. Had hoped in the first lesson to touch on Meditation; however, when I went up to Mrs Hodges afterwards and asked her to give me a mantra she seemed positively baffled and said, 'Do you mean a lift home?' I think she must have taken me for a foreigner.

Arrived back at the flat, bathed and cleaned my teeth, and went into the sitting room to practice my lotus position in front of 'News at Ten'. Chimes of Big Ben scarcely died away when the most excruciating pain shot through my knee. Lept to my feet and hobbled on to the sofa where I lay staring alternately at Sandy Gall and my knee. I do not know which gave me less pleasure.

To bed finally in great pain, where I chose a suitably obscene mantra which I repeated over and over again until falling into an uneasy sleep.

Friday, October 27th

Knee still stiff – not that my fellow tube travellers apparently cared two hoots. Not one of them offered to give up his seat, despite my obvious limp. Humanity seems to be as much a thing of the past as manners.

So that joint should not stiffen up unduly, strolled to

nearest bookshop for a bit of a browse. Came upon a fascinating book about finger massage, which is like acupuncture but without the needles. Apparently all you have to do is locate the pressure point that corresponds to the area of the body where the pain is, then press down on it with the point of your finger, jiggle it about a bit and the pain disappears.

Looked up 'Pain in the Knee' and found that relevant point is three fingers width above top of patella on the outer side of the thigh. Turned my back on the other customers, quickly rolled up trouser leg and followed instructions as per book. Was beginning to experience definite relief when there was a tap on my shoulder. Straightened up to be confronted by shop manager who said, 'I don't know what you are doing and I don't much care, but whatever it is I'd be glad if you would not do it in my shop.' Needless to say, one or two customers started sniggering and whispering together. I looked the fellow straight in the eye and said, 'There was a time when it was considered normal practice to test the quality of goods before purchase, but perhaps I'm very old-fashioned.'

'Yes,' said the manager, 'you are.'

I replied that in that case it was a pity there weren't a few more old-fashioned people about, adding that it was most unethical of him to be offering manuals of this sort for sale on the open shelves without allowing customers the opportunity to test their efficiency.

He said, 'I suppose the next thing you'll be wanting is to bring your girlfriend in to try out *The Joy of Sex*.'

The trouble with the shopkeeper mentality is that it never knows where to draw the line. Had no intention of buying book after that and told him so. Took bus to Foyles only to find they were out of stock, so compelled to return to original shop after all.

Got home to find that the GPO had been to install the jack for my answering machine. It's only taken nine weeks.

Saturday, October 28th

Hooray, hooray. At last I've got my answering machine. The man came to install it this morning and spent a good twenty minutes showing me how to get the best from the service.

I do see that a cheerful, friendly, perhaps even slightly apologetic message is preferable to the brusquer, more formal type of greeting. Have decided to aim for an approach somewhere between the two. Charm without sycophancy should be the keynote, I think.

Spent the afternoon thinking up a suitable message which, after several bosh shots, I have finally recorded. Set machine and popped out to buy a few groceries. Returned to find no one had left any messages, but decided to leave it on anyway. I had a feeling Pippa might ring and I certainly did not wish to give the impression that I have nothing better to do on Saturdays than sit at home. Later, on an impulse, drove round to Parson's Green to find a note pinned to the door from Amanda saying she had been trying to ring me all afternoon to suggest going to the Woody Allen film, but had given up and gone out instead with Christopher.

Realized something must be wrong with the machine and rushed home to find I had left dial on wrong position. Re-set it and nipped out for some eggs before the shops shut. Got back to discover someone had called. Re-wound tape only to hear a long silence followed by the receiver being replaced. I suspect it was Pippa, but there's no way I can be sure, short of ringing up, and that would ruin the whole effect. A wretched evening. And who is this Christopher when he's at home?

Sunday, October 29th

A sleepless night, filled with doubts and anxieties. Have listed them in order of concern. I always think problems are easier to consider once they are down on paper. I suppose that's the writer in me coming out again.

Many people, faced with so many unsolved dilemmas tend to let matters sort themselves out of their own accord. I prefer a more positive attitude myself. Like Lord Mountbatten, I am a man of action and, as such, believe in taking life by the scruff of its neck and shaking it, as a dog shakes a rat. Of course it is bound to be unpleasant, and people are liable to get hurt in the process, but better that than a slow decline into a morass of indifference and inertia.

I shall begin straight away by sorting out this wretched headache that has been plaguing me since breakfast. The pressure point, I see from my finger massage book, is on the inside of one's wrist.

Monday, October 30th

Headache completely cured, but I now have an extremely sore wrist.

Morning post brings a copy of the most recent register of OFs, plus an invoice for £3.75, not including VAT. I was outraged, though not half as much as I was to find that my name is not included. Not that I could care less whether I am in there or not. It's just that the whole thing's so hopelessly incomplete. National Theatre actor also not included. But then I might have expected that.

Have written off to the secretary of the OF society, registering my complaint in the strongest possible terms and returning his insulting invoice. Father did not pay all that money in 1960 to make me a life member for nothing. No messages on the answering machine this evening.

Tuesday, October 31st

Rang Hugh early. Before I could utter a word he said, 'Whatever were you thinking of when you recorded that message for your machine? You sound like some terrible old poof.'

I said coldly, 'I can only think there is something wrong with your telephone,' and hung up on him.

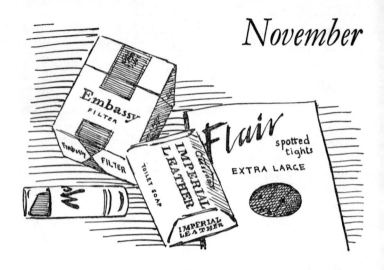

November

Wednesday, November 1st

Have been reading the famous cases of Sir Patrick Hastings. I realize that great advocacy is a thing of the past, but a well-argued, well-delivered speech, concentrating on my hitherto impeccable record, can certainly do me no harm. As soon as they see the sort of person they are dealing with I feel sure they will simply let me off with a warning.

On the way home had my hair cut extra short.

Later hunted my old school black jacket and pin-striped trousers out of mothballs and tried them on. Stood in front of mirror and in Churchillian style, seized my lapels, one of which came clean away in my hand.

I think the grey double-breasted with the chalk stripe will do just as well.

Thursday, November 2nd

Was skimming through OF news on loo this morning when my eye alighted on the name of Dishforth. He was a House Runt in School House at the same time as me, and for a couple of semesters we shared a cubby together. I never realized until now that his name was David. He was always known throughout the school as Dirty – for all the obvious reasons.

Typical of him to think that anyone would wish to know

what he has been up to for the last eighteen years. He always was pushy. Slightly Jewish if I remember rightly.

He is now a successful solicitor in Theobalds Road. On an impulse, rang him from the office to sound him out on my chances with the West London Magistrates. He listened politely while I outlined the facts of the case, then said, 'Are you asking for my professional advice?' I said that I certainly was.

He said, 'I'd try the human weakness ploy myself – ' he said. 'Say that you were driving along quite normally at about 20 m.p.h. when suddenly you were gripped by the most appalling attack of the trots. Naturally you needed to get home as quickly as possible for fear of soiling the upholstery.'

I said that if I'd known he was going to be so flippant, I'd never have rung him.'

He said, 'I'm being perfectly serious.'

'In that case,' I said, 'I'd *seriously* advise you to consider another profession. Like writing BBC comedy scripts.'

'Oh, I do that already,' he said. 'in my spare time of course.'

Could not resist remarking that there was no mention of this in the OF news.

'Maybe not,' he said, 'but at least I pay my debts.'

When I asked him what that was supposed to mean, he replied that I owed the society £3.75 plus VAT for a copy of the OF register.

I replied that, if it was any of his business, I was a life member and, as such, was not obliged to pay for registers.

He said, 'It *is* my business. I happen to be the new honorary secretary. And what's more, you're not a member, life or anything else. You resigned from the society six months ago.'

Friday, November 3rd

Woke with a shock to realize that I had forgotten to cancel my yoga classes. It's always a great mistake to pay for things in advance these days: there's always some good reason why you shouldn't get your money back.

Rang Mrs Hodges who said, 'I am not surprised that you didn't come back.'

When I asked her why, she said, 'Some people are serious about this sort of thing, some aren't.'

I said that, if she really wanted to know, I'd given my knee a very nasty wrench, thanks to her.

'Your excuses,' she said, 'are your own affair.'

I'd had enough of beating about the bush.

'I suppose there's no chance of my getting a refund?' I said.

'The more I think about it,' Mrs Hodges said, 'the more I think you were right to give up yoga. You're far too aggressive.'

The trouble with these left-wing, pacifist, self-improvement merchants is that one can never get a straight answer out of them.

Bumped into Pippa in lift after lunch.

She said 'Have you seen the Hills lately?'

I said that I hadn't and, more to the point, when was I going to see her again?

'You see me every day,' she said.

Why is it that everything I say nowadays is automatically misinterpreted?

Saturday, November 4th

Woken early by the phone. A voice said 'Is that Mr Crisp?' I said that it was. 'Simon Crisp?' asked the voice. I repeated that that was so. 'Oh, I'm so sorry,' said the voice, 'I wanted to speak to his answering machine,' and put the phone down.

Is it my imagination, or did it sound remarkably like Beddoes?

To the Pedalows in the evening for dinner with Amanda. Theresa and Philippe de Grande-Hauteville there. They can talk about nothing but their wretched baby. I suppose it's understandable, their being so much older than the average first-time parent. He now seems convinced that I work in Fleet Street. I could not be bothered to disillusion him.

She looking greyer than I remember.

Good conversation at dinner, mainly about the adaptation of this famous spy novel on television. I seem to be the only one who thinks it has the slightest merit. As I told Tim, the whole point about spying is that in real life it is a very slow, methodical business.

'I don't want reality', he said, 'I want entertainment.'

As an epitaph on the Pedalow gravestone it could hardly be bettered.

During coffee, Tim left the room and came back with a bag of golf clubs. He extracted a seven iron, unscrewed the head and slid out a long, thin packet which he carefully unwrapped and, amid much oohing and aaahing from the others, proceeded to make up a cigarette. With one rap hanging over my head already, I was not going to risk getting busted and, when it came to my turn to have a puff, I said, 'I happen to know a thing or two about addiction,' and passed it on.

Felt quite dizzy on the way home. I put it down to all those fumes amidst which I was forced to spend the last hour of an otherwise quite enjoyable evening.

Sunday, November 5th

The great mystery has at last been uncovered. Christopher is a dog – to be precise, a large white Pyrenean Mountain dog.

It belongs to A's antique-dealer friend Brian and his boy friend, and A looks after it when they go off for their weekends in Amsterdam.

Am not a great lover of dogs, least of all the type that rush at you the moment you open the front door, hurl their paws against your chest, then slide down, pulling great lengths of wool out of your pullover.

Had been hoping, in the light of Pippa's lack of enthusiasm, to take the dying embers of our fading love affair and coax them into flame.

Suggested to Amanda that we might spend tomorrow lunchtime looking for an engagement ring. Anyone would have thought I'd suggested a hiking holiday in the Andes from the astonished look on her face.

'An engagement ring?' she exclaimed. 'Who for?'

'For you, of course,' I told her. 'Who else?'

'You and me?' she said. 'Engaged? You're not serious.'

I replied that I had never been more serious in my life, and that I was sorry it had taken me so long to make up my mind, but that I have never believed in rushing into things. To my amazement, she burst into shrieks of laughter.

'What ever makes you think I'd want to *marry* you?' she said. I replied stiffly that I was aware that for us the path of true love had certainly not run as smooth as it might have done, but that, as far as I was aware, there had always been an understanding between us.

She said, 'The only thing I understood was that we were friends – you have obviously been expecting something more.'

I said, 'Are you trying to tell me it's all off?'

'Poor old Simon,' she said. 'It was never really on, was it?' Not for her perhaps; it certainly was for me. Still, there seemed no purpose in labouring the point, and we've left it that I'll call her in a few days. We both need time to think things over.

She said, 'It won't do any good.'

'We'll see, we'll see.' I suppose that, if I were really honest with myself, I'd have to admit I've seen this coming for some time, but now that it has, it is no easier to bear. All in all, the worst Guy Fawkes Night I can remember in a very long time.

Monday, November 6th

The most wretched start to a week I've ever known. However, the morning post brought a letter from Beddoes proposing a trip to Brussels next weekend.

Surprised to realize how much I have missed him in recent weeks. For all his bad behaviour, he is a lively companion and although we do not see eye-to-eye on moral matters, a completely fresh approach to the vexed question of my emotional and sexual life could be just what's needed. On a more serious note, I am deeply concerned over our contribution to the Common Market budget; one's knowledge of the workings of the EEC is all too sketchy and I welcome this opportunity to acquaint myself with this organization into whose hands we have so blithely committed ourselves.

Rang the European Commission HQ from the office, but no one on the switchboard seemed to have heard of Monsieur Ralph Beddoes.

Unfortunately, I was unable to give them the slightest clue as to his function, and my assurance that he is something of a big cheese led predictably to much confusion.

Finally ran him to earth this evening at his flat. He was obviously delighted to hear that I was coming and doubly so that I would be alone. Knowing him, I daresay he's laid on a couple of loose women. *Tant mieux.*

Tuesday, November 7th

Feel I cannot let personal feelings interfere with my responsibilities towards the Conservative party, and think I may have come up with a perfect fund-raising idea. A real 1950s dance, just like the ones we always used to go to as teenagers during the school holidays. Dancing 8.30 to 1.00. Cold buffet with wine cup. A real old-fashioned eight-piece band. Quicksteps and slow quicksteps, waltzes and valetas, Gay Gordons and Dashing White Sergeants and Strip the Willow, and, of course, the Last Waltz with the lights dimmed. A Teenage Dance. It will be a sell-out. All I need now is a committee to help me organize it. Got on the phone as soon as I arrived in the office and have already co-opted Tim and Vanessa Pedalow and Theresa de Grande Hauteville. Philippe, being foreign, obviously wouldn't understand.

Terribly tempted to ask Jane Baker to help. It's very much her thing. And so, the more I think about it, am I.

Wednesday, November 8th

Rang Jane and she has said yes. We have fixed our first committee meeting for a week today.

To my nearest travel agent at lunchtime to book an economy return flight to Brussels. Unfortunately, have left it far too late and must pay full fare of £99. At those prices, is it any wonder we can't afford to stay in the EEC? On the other hand, if one cannot splash out at my age, when can one?

To the wine tasting in the evening with Tim, in a cellar somewhere off Lombard Street.

Wines in question all Burgundies from the Chambolle-Musigny region, wherever that might be. Asked Tim who said, 'What does it matter *where* it is? It's *what* it is that matters.'

Whether he actually knows anything about wine is hard to tell. At all events, he made a great fuss, sticking his nose into the glass, sloshing the stuff from cheek to cheek and smacking his lips after each swallow.

As far as I was concerned, they all tasted exactly the same. Tim said that, in his view, wine was meant to be drunk, not to be spat out into barrels of sawdust. I replied that if I had swallowed every glass I had tasted, I'd be under the table by now.

'It depends what you're used to,' he said, throwing back his head for the umpteenth time.

Oddly enough although not a single drop passed my throat, by the time we left at half-past-nine, the room was reeling and Tim had to help me into a taxi.

Had intended to spend the evening preparing my speech for the trial tomorrow, but collapsed on to the bed where I fell fast asleep and dreamt that I was Sir Patrick Hastings defending Tim Pedalow on a drunken driving charge, and losing.

Thursday, November 9th

Woke at six-thirty feeling dreadful. Bathed and dressed in dark grey with chalk stripe.

Arrived at court shortly before ten. How ironic life can be: the last time I set foot in such a place it was very much on the other side of the legal fence, as a juror.

Surprised to note how few of my fellow defendants had bothered to dress for the occasion.

Gave my name to the clerk and went to sit on a bench with my fellow criminals. Normally would not have bothered to pass the time of day with such types, but crime is a great leveller and it would have been a narrow-minded man indeed who did not welcome this opportunity of an insight into the mentality of the criminal classes.

One, a coloured man, said he reckoned he'd get eighteen months and another said he'd rather get a short stretch than a fine any day as he always forgot to pay them and finished up in the nick anyway.

Fascinated to find how quickly and easily one falls in with the criminal argot and way of thinking. I said, 'On balance, I prefer a fine.'

'What you up for then?' the coloured man asked me. I said casually, 'Oh, a little bit of this and that. You know,' and tapped the side of my nose and winked.

Soon began to wish I really were up on a more serious charge. For some reason all the others were summoned before me and it was midday when my name was finally called.

Found myself face to face with two pleasant-looking elderly men in dark suits and a grey-haired woman. The charge was read out and I was asked if I had anything to say.

Made, I think, a very good speech: succinct, witty and not too flowery.

The chairman said, 'Very interesting,' and began to confer with his colleagues in a low voice.

Finally, he looked up and said, 'If you had a real excuse to offer – you suddenly felt ill or something – I might have understood. As it is, fined forty pounds and licence endorsed.'

On way down to accounts office, asked the usher how forty rated as fines went.

'About average,' he said.

Said nothing but could not help thinking that if I hadn't shown up in person, it might have been a good deal stiffer.

Was crossing the road when I bumped into my coloured friend.

He asked me what I'd got and when I told him, he said, 'Bad luck. Next time try damage to property. I got six months suspended. See you,' and walked jauntily up the street. To rob a bank, no doubt.

Is there no justice?

Am seriously considering taking the matter up with my MP. Whoever he may be.

Friday, November 10th

Arrived home last night to find a most curious message on my machine.

'Mr Crisp,' said the voice. 'I hope you have a very enjoyable weekend.'

Laughed it off as a jape by one of my friends and went to bed.

Woke at four in a muck sweat, convinced that some lunatic had planted a bomb on the 9.30 plane to Brussels and was ringing up every one of the passengers to gloat.

Lay there sleepless till eight when I rang the airline to ask if it was possible for anyone to get hold of a copy of the passenger list.

The girl said it was out of the question, but I was taking no risks. Told them to cancel my reservation and rang British Rail to find that the boat train was leaving at ten.

Rang Beddoes to tell him of change of plan. Debated whether to leave his number on answering machine in case of emergency but finally decided against it. One doesn't want to make it any easier for burglars than it already is.

Rushed to Victoria and caught the train by seconds. Felt oddly like the Duke of Windsor going into exile.

Crossing delayed by an hour owing to bomb scare, but once under way the journey passed quickly enough. A pity it was rough. People are so stupid. If only they'd get out on deck, they'd feel 100 per cent better straight away. I certainly did. Of course, there are always exceptions – viz. the Indian next to me by the lifeboat. I suppose it was my fault for standing down-wind of him, but that did not make a faceful of regurgitated curry any more palatable.

Finally arrived at Brussels station at 9 p.m.

No sign of Beddoes. Ring his flat. Girl answers. Ralph will be there soon. Half an hour later, no Ralph. Phone again. Same girl: he's been delayed. Twenty minutes later, he rolls up in a large grey Mercedes, 'Hope I haven't kept you waiting, laddie.' Snigger, snigger 'Spot of unfinished business.' Snigger, snigger. 'We thought we'd all go out to eat somewhere, then perhaps go on to a club and meet some friends then back to my place for a night cap. . . .'

I'm sorry to be a wet blanket, but there it is. As Beddoes' Dutch live-in girlfriend, Lola, points out, we have the whole weekend ahead of us, but he won't have it. European life seems to have made him, if anything, worse.

Saturday, November 11th

A late start.

To Waterloo after lunch to view famous battlefield. A fitting outing on Remembrance weekend. Lola extremely knowledgeable about the battle. She took us first to La Belle Alliance, the inn on the far hill that Napoleon used as his HQ, thence down the valley to Hougoumont, the famous farm, so valiantly and decisively defended by the Scots Guards. Not for the first time, I found myself wondering if there is a single country in the world whose tourist industry does not owe its success to British courage, skill and initiative. Travel certainly broadens the chest.

Drove to the Lion Monument for final panoramic view of

field of battle. The huge mound, surmounted by a large lion, stands on the very spot from which the Iron Duke directed the proceedings. Arrived just as attendant with moth-eaten moustache was locking the gateway to this magnificent memorial to courage and patriotism. Reminded him in no uncertain terms who won this battle, but he shrugged his shoulders and plodded off into the gathering gloom. 'If it hadn't been for people like us,' I called out after him, 'there wouldn't be a monument for you to guard.'

'Actually,' said Lola, 'the monument was erected in memory of the Prince of Orange, son of the King of Holland.'

Even if she was right, there was no reason to be quite so smug.

Dined at the most lively fish restaurant behind the Grande Place.

Halfway through my second plate of mussels when Beddoes said, 'Hallo, you're in luck. Here's one of our Commissioners. You may not realize it in England but he is probably one of the most important men in the world right now.'

Noticed a slight hush descend over the proceedings.

As the Commissioner and his party passed our table he paused briefly and said a few words to Beddoes who in turn introduced me.

I stood up, opened my mouth to speak and belched loudly.

The Commissioner said, 'Enjoying your mussels, I see,' and passed on his way.

Beddoes said, 'Bang go our chances of being asked to dinner there.'

I said I was very sorry, but if one's career in Europe hung on a belch, then that was about all it was worth anyway.

Beddoes said 'Then that just shows how little you people in England understand about the EEC.'

I suggested that the Commissioner had probably never even noticed.

Beddoes said, 'People like that do not get where they are by not noticing things.'

To bed on a slightly frosty note. *Plus ça change.*

Sunday, November 12th

To Bruges for the day. A most fascinating medieval city. According to Lola, it is known as the Venice of the North.

Could not resist remarking that I had yet to hear of Venice being described as the Bruges of the South.

Dinner in the flat, cooked by Lola, and very nice too. Over coffee, I suggested to Beddoes that he might care to give me the low-down on this Common Agricultural Policy row.

He thought for a moment and said, 'I'd like to show you something.'

Leaving Lola with the washing-up, we got into the car and drove down a sidestreet where a number of girls sat in lighted windows, knitting scarves and flipping through magazines.

Beddoes told me, as if I hadn't guessed already, that this was the red-light district.

For an awful moment I was afraid he was going to suggest sampling the wares, but he seemed content to drive up one street and down the next, making lewd and suggestive comments as we went. It was all most embarrassing, especially as we got caught up in a one-way system and found ourselves driving up and down the same two streets half a dozen times looking for the way out. By the end, some of the girls had actually started waving at us and making provocative signs in our direction. We finally extricated ourselves and as we drove home I said to Beddoes, 'Most interesting, but I'm afraid the metaphor escapes me. What has all that to do with the Common Agricultural Policy?'

'Nothing whatever,' he said. 'I just thought you'd be interested, that's all.'

Is it any wonder the Prime Minister is having such problems achieving credibility with Schmidt and Giscard when this is the sort of back-up she has to rely on.

Monday, November 13th

Entire day spent travelling. Remarked to one of the old stewards on the boat that I felt sure in the old days, when the rich travelled to the Continent by boat, it was all much more comfortable.

'It still is,' he said, 'if you travel on the night sleeper.'

Typical of my travel agent not to have thought of suggesting it.

Arrived back at the flat to find several messages on the machine: from Pratt asking why I wasn't at the reps meeting, from Enid saying when could I give her the names of the committee, from Tim saying would I call him and from Mother wondering whether I'd made my mind up yet about Christmas. Nothing from Amanda.

Also a bill from Dirty Dishforth – 'To professional services' – £25, of all the cheek.

I definitely remember now that he had a Jewish mother.

Tuesday, November 14th

Tackled Pratt first thing. I have always believed that the best form of defence is attack, and said that, if he thought a reps meeting was more important to Barfords than an exchange of views with a European Commissioner then he might just as well start looking for a new deputy.

He said, 'I think you might have let me in on your plans.'

'There are occasions,' I said, 'in this fast-moving world of modern business, where one simply has to seize ones chances as and when they occur.'

It's this sort of petty-fogging, small-mindedness that is responsible for Britain's poor performance in world markets today.

He grudgingly conceded I might have a point. I somehow don't think we shall be hearing from that quarter for quite some time.

Had not considered it before, but I see no reason now why I should not claim at least part of my trip on expenses.

Tim rang after lunch to say that he and Vanessa had been planning a weekend trip to Moscow on Saturday week, but that she had walked out on him in Annabel's on Friday night and would I care to go in her place. I have long held the view that in this day and age no one can speak with authority about modern political life without first having visited America and Russia. To be offered the opportunity of experiencing the two extremes of the political spectrum in as many months is one that no thinking man would dream of refusing. Have told Tim I'll think about it and call him back tomorrow.

New York, Brussels, Moscow: where will it all end?

There's no doubt this is my year for seeing the world and the more my life expands, the more convinced I am that even to consider tying myself down to a married life at this exciting stage of my career would be sheer madness. I am now convinced that the break with Amanda is a blessing in disguise.

On to Moscow. I wonder if there's a potential market for Barfords there? What a feather in my cap that would be! Have made a note to write a memo to Hardacre on the subject.

Wednesday, November 15th

Rang Tim first thing to say I am definitely on for Russia. I thought he seemed most relieved. Am a firm believer in doing my homework before visiting a country for the first time, so walked to the library at lunchtime to borrow a copy of *Das Kapital*. It is a good deal larger than I had imagined, and heavier. Was glad I had the sense to take a plastic carrier bag with me, even though the handle did break on the way back. I already have the reputation at the office for being a bit of an intellectual and with all this talk of traitors at the palace I wouldn't put it past any of my colleagues to leap to the conclusion that they have a mole in their midst. Put book away in drawer and forgot all about it until I arrived home. Rang office, but no reply. Drove round, but place locked and in darkness. I don't know why I am worrying. No one ever comes to my office in daytime, so it's hardly likely they'd suddenly start doing so in the middle of the night.

Thursday, November 16th

Arrived at office at seven-thirty. Book apparently untouched – ditto waste paper basket and dirty coffee cup.

Posted off passport to travel company. I hope there's not going to be any trouble *vis-à-vis* my American visa. (Rather a good joke that.)

To Pedalows after work for inaugural committee meeting. Tim clearly relishing his new bachelor status as much as I am. Jane completely transformed, I hardly recognized her. Her skin has quite cleared up and she has given up those dreadful glasses in favour of soft contact lenses. She has even taken to wearing a little make-up. I could not take my eyes off her. Delighted to hear that she had at last given Armitage the boot. I said, 'We must get together again soon.'

'I don't think that will be possible,' she said, 'now that I'm engaged to Hugo.'

Life is all a matter of timing.

Everyone very keen on my Teenage Dance idea, although we wasted far too much time persuading Theresa that a Beautiful Baby Contest just isn't on. While I am delighted that she and Philippe have found happiness together in middle age and I do appreciate that their baby is very special to them, it isn't to everyone.

I also think that if one must bring a child to a committee meeting, one really ought to be able to think up better ways of stopping it grizzling than opening one's blouse and breast-feeding it. Natural rearing may be all the rage now but do we have to have it shoved down our throats?

It simply isn't the sort of thing one expects of Young Conservatives.

All in all, though, a most successful meeting. Tim has agreed to organize the band and the hall; Jane will do the food; Theresa is in charge of decorations; I will handle public relations and advertising.

It was unfortunate that Theresa had to come across my copy of Marx just as we were leaving. She claimed she was looking for the disposable nappies.

'What's this?' she cried, 'A traitor in our midst?'

I said coolly 'He is a foolish man indeed who rides into battle without first knowing the mind of the enemy.' Everyone laughed and the tension dissolved.

Tim said laughingly, 'That was very good. Just like Philby at his press conference in '55. You'd make a jolly good mole.'

Friday, November 17th

Is it my imagination or was the same man who got on the tube with me at Holland Park this morning still behind me as I walked down Chancery Lane? I also have the impression that there are many more clicks and buzzes than usual on my telephone, and have therefore taken to speaking through a handkerchief. As for Tim's joke last night about Philby and my making a good mole, I am not a fanciful man, but I have a definite feeling he was trying to tell me something. In fact the more I think about it, the more convinced I am that there is more to this Russian trip than meets the eye. It would not surprise me one little bit to learn that Tim is a talent spotter for the Russians. He has the perfect background: public school, Cambridge, etc., and perfect cover: respectable job in the City, entailing a certain amount of travel. What more could the KGB ask? Quite why he should consider me as a possible agent, I cannot imagine. I neither drink nor am I homosexual. Nor, on the other hand, am I in the habit of expressing dissatisfaction with the *status quo* or sympathy with Mr Brezhnev and his cronies.

I am wondering if the fact that I enjoyed that spy series on TV so much has anything to do with it. It's tiny dropped hints of this sort that spymasters seize on without one realizing it.

Could call Tim's bluff, of course, and make it quite clear from the word go that it's just not on, but on reflection think I'll bide my time and see how the land lies.

Softly, softly, catchee molee.

Saturday, November 18th

Tried to read *Das Kapital* in bed last night, but somehow just couldn't get into it. In the end fell asleep with the tome resting on my chest. Woke up in the small hours with the light still on and quite a pain in my chest.

Mollie rang after breakfast to say that she had received some details from an estate agent for a house which boasted, among other things, a 'vehicle hard-standing.' She seemed to think that highly amusing.

Tried to avoid telling her about Russia but it slipped out anyway.

She said, 'Well, all I can say is, they don't wear those fur hats for nothing.'

When I asked her to elaborate, she explained that since 80 per cent of one's body temperature escapes through the top of one's head, a fur hat in those sub-zero temperatures was very much a *sine qua non*.

The trouble with people who have hot air coming through the tops of their heads, whatever the temperature, is that one can never be entirely sure when they are telling the truth. However, I have always rather fancied myself in fur ever since Mr Macmillan went to see Mr Khrushchev. Hurried off to the shops to see what they had in stock. Was trying one on in Harrods when Tim appeared from nowhere and said, 'Don't buy a fur hat here. They have the real thing in Moscow at half the price.'

Now how did he know that if he's never been before?

And was it really plain coincidence that he should be in Harrods at exactly the same time as me?

The plot thickens.

Sunday, November 19th

To Mother's for lunch – possibly the last we shall have together. On the way down, heard a fascinating talk on the wireless on how to barbecue an entire pig.

Mother quite unconcerned about my escapade behind the Iron Curtain. All she said was, 'I hope this doesn't mean you'll be away for Christmas.'

I may be away for a great many Christmases if I don't play my cards very carefully indeed, but said nothing to her.

As I was leaving she said, 'Just make sure you wrap up warm. I don't want you going down with a cold just before Christmas.' Talk about a one-track mind.

Monday, November 20th

Took *Das Kapital* back to library on way in to work. With the best will in the world I am quite unable to get beyond page two. Goodness knows how Marx thought the uneducated masses were going to lap it up. Anyway, to my way of thinking, if one cannot get the flavour of a society by living amongst the people for a few days, one's certainly not going to get it from books.

Memo from Keith Hardacre concerning my memo to him, to the effect that likelihood of trading agreement with Russians extremely remote. On no account am I to repeat my foolish behaviour in Brussels by trying to take things into my own hands. Nothing, repeat, nothing should be undertaken on behalf of the company by any junior executive without the prior consent of a board member, and then only under the strictest supervision. Not even Christina Onassis can do as she likes and she owns her company, etc. etc.

I have never been so insulted. Am I Deputy Marketing Manager or am I some pipsqueak of no more importance than an office boy?

Rang Keith and put the question to him straight from the shoulder. He said, 'As far as this sort of thing is concerned, you are a pipsqueak of no more importance than an office boy.'

Is there no place left in Britain these days for flair and initiative? Has the lesson of my Brussels trip still not got through? For two pins I'd emigrate somewhere where my talents are really appreciated and nurtured. Possibly Russia.

Tuesday, November 21st

A disastrous start to the day.

Had dressed, shaved, breakfasted, etc. and was just on way out when I discovered hands still slightly sticky with marmalade.

Went to wash them under bath tap, owing to underpants soaking in basin. Unfortunately, had forgotten to switch knob from shower to bath and turned on tap to receive powerful jet of water on top of head. Hair completely soaked, also shirt, tie and jacket.

As a result, stepped out of front door considerably later than planned. Looked down to see small brown package leaning against door frame. Closer examination revealed that it was postmarked SW11 – a favourite haunt of anarchists and parcel-post bombers if I'm not mistaken. Also noticed my name spelt wrong. I suppose it could have been perfectly innocent, but one cannot afford to take any risks these days. It is quite possible that my name is down on someone's death list. Hurried indoors at once and rang the police.

I imagine they must be the victims of many hoaxes in the course of their work but obviously they believed this to be the real thing since they were round in less than an hour.

Have told them I am available to answer questions until Friday evening, but did not mention Russia. Also suggested making a list of possible enemies.

They said it's not necessary, but I think I'll do it anyway.

Wednesday, November 22nd

No news yet from the police. My own list of suspects shorter than I had imagined. Am curiously disappointed.

Thinking of *bêtes noires*, I see from today's *Times* that Sir Peter Hall is 49. I suppose it's the beard that makes him look older.

Also noticed that Professor K. B. S. Smellie is 82.

I wonder if he is any relation to Andrew Smellie who was so anxious we should be kept *au courant* with his career in the last but one OF news? I'm quite sorry now I chucked in my membership. I'd really have something to set my contemporaries by their ears in the next edition.

Thursday, November 23rd

Tim rang with the stunning news that he will not now be coming to Russia after all, since Vanessa has come back and they have decided to have a week's holiday in Istanbul to celebrate, but that he hoped I'd received the packet of guide books and leaflets he'd sent on Monday.

He said, 'Sorry to let you down at the last minute, but I think you'll find you'll be very well looked after.'

By his controller at the Centre, no doubt.

Friday, November 24th

Passport returned in morning post, plus visa. No query about my trip to America I notice. Parcel of leaflets returned by police.

A sudden ghastly thought occurred to me on the way to work. If Tim does do something silly, I shall have to find someone else to arrange the band and hall for the Teenage Dance.

Despite earlier rudeness on the subject, rang Bryant-Fenn to sound him out as a possible substitute.

Before I could get a word out, he said, 'I hear you're off to Moscow.'

Hedged slightly at first, but finally he wheedled the truth out of me.

'One word of advice, old man,' he said. 'Take plenty of gifts for the natives. It's the only way you'll get anything done. But, of course, I don't need to tell that to a well-travelled chap like you.'

Frankly, it was all gobbledygook to me. I said, 'No, of course not. What sort of gifts do *you* take?'

He said, 'Oh, the usual things you know: soap, chewing gum, fags, lipstick, chocolate, of course. I gather Pentel pens go down very well these days, and tights – the larger the better, knowing Russian women.'

While I have no intention of being arrested for smuggling before I've even got into the country, I have heard that it is hard to get certain goods in Russia, so perhaps the authorities turn a blind eye to this system of tipping. The problem is, how much of everything to take? Is one bar of Imperial Leather enough to ensure early morning tea and how many pairs of tights does one need for a seat at the Bolshoi?

Have decided to err on the side of generosity and take more than one really needs.

I only hope I've got the right shade of lipstick. The girl assured me that Morning Rose is very popular.

Before leaving this evening, fired off memo to the office manager asking for the name on my door to be altered a.s.a.p. I only hope it will be worth the effort.

Saturday, November 25th

Arrived at London Airport in good time for noon flight. Rest of the party the usual unlikely mixture of age and class one invariably meets on package tours. Not that I have been on that many, of course.

One quite glamorous blonde girl with a fur coat and suede boots. She is alone, but why? Tried to wangle seat next to her on flight, but edged out by tough looking, grey-haired man in sheepskin coat and corduroy suit.

They're obviously all set for a bit of a thing. I think I may have missed the boat there.

Landed up next to elderly woman named Mrs Antrobus whose son, she claimed, had been a contemporary of mine at Oxford. The name means nothing. I gather he was very keen on madrigal singing.

She said, 'Do I gather this is your first visit?' I said it was. 'It's always exciting the first time,' she said. 'This is my fifth.'

Opened my brief-case to take out my *Guide Bleu*. Mrs Antrobus took one look at the array of lipsticks, soap, etc. and exclaimed, 'Aha, a commercial traveller!' Tried to explain about tipping but nothing I said could persuade her otherwise. I can see that I am going to be stuck with the nickname 'The Traveller' for the rest of the weekend.

Long, unexplained delay at Moscow Airport while our

Intourist guide, Irena, scurried about in an aimless sort of way. Finally shepherded on to ancient bus for long, cold drive across flat empty countryside to city.

Tim's not going to like this after a lifetimes' weekending in the Cotswolds. Finally drew up at Metropole, a large, once plush Edwardian hotel, just off Red Square.

Key-lady on my landing excessively grim despite my cheery greeting. Shall obviously have to slip her something straight away, but what? And how awful if she were to refuse – or worse, send for the police. Hung about in corridor to see if anyone else slipped her anything, but decided it doesn't do to draw attention to oneself in Communist countries.

Bedroom spartan in the extreme – torn curtains and no bath plug. Hugh was right about bringing a squash ball. I assumed he was joking. Who wouldn't?

Room far too hot for my taste, so threw open window while unpacking. Temperature soon dropped owing to sub-zero conditions outside. Unfortunately, unable to close window again, and had to wedge it with *Times*. Hunted for a while for bug, but without success. Suddenly overwhelmed by conviction that mirror on wall two-way. Covered it with towel and dismantled telephone. Not knowing what inside of Russian telephone looks like normally, impossible to tell if bug inserted or not. Struggled to put it together but failed. Reassembled it as best as I could and went down to dinner.

Marinated fish, meat, potatoes and dry cake, washed down with sweet fizzy drink like Lucozade, in an echoing barn of a room, watched over by glowering waitresses.

Sat next to large girl with blonde hair who said, 'You look the sort of man who knows what's what.' I did not disagree. Her name is Belinda Bott. Rather apt. She has managed to work out that she and her ex-husband were also at Oxford at the same time as me. Am beginning to wonder if there is anyone in Moscow who wasn't.

When I asked her which college she was at, she said, 'Balliol.' Naturally I expressed surprise. 'Strictly night-time only,' she said and guffawed loudly. If I had a name like Belinda Bott, I think I'd keep very quiet indeed.

After dinner went up to third floor to look at Berioska Tourist shop which was closed. Arrived back in my room to discover that someone had closed the window, also put telephone together. Interesting. To bed humming 'Midnight in Moscow'.

Sunday, November 26th

Spotted curious protuberance high up on wall I had not noticed before. Will investigate later.

After breakfast hurried up to Berioska shop to find several shelves of fur hats. Toyed with silver fox and astrakhan, but finally plumped for more typical rabbit fur. A bargain, to my mind, at 9 roubles 20 kopeks, and a perfect fit. Astonished to find that one can pay with American Express. I'm only sorry I didn't bring my card. However, pound notes equally welcome.

Morning spent on general sight-seeing tour of city. Blonde girl and grey-haired man together again, I was sorry to see. She is rather my type. Her name is Angela and his is Ken. Did my best to avoid Belinda Bott, but without success.

'That's a nice hat,' she boomed as she slumped beside me on the coach, crushing my thigh. 'Pity about the white patch.'

I had not noticed it before, but now she mentioned it, it stood out in a most irritating fashion so that I could scarcely think of anything else all morning. Caught Irena staring at me several times during lunch.

Returned to Berioska and explained my problem re hat. Assistant in grey suit shook his head, indicating that, since he had already snipped the label from the hat, any exchange was now out of the question. I suggested he could always thread it back through, but he was not to be persuaded.

Suddenly had a brilliant thought. Snatched my Pentel pen from my pocket and thrust it into his hand. He nodded his thanks and put the gift in his pocket. Assuming that I now had the go-ahead to take the new hat, I picked it up and made to leave, but he rushed forward and seized it from me, and an undignified tussle ensued. Out of the corner of my eye I noticed his colleague picking up the telephone and dialling.

Decided to cut my losses and make a run for it. Mentioned my problem to Irena as we were getting on to bus for after-noon outing to Kolomenskoye Palace and she said if I left it with her she would see what she could do.

At dinner she arrived carrying paper bag containing new

hat. Thanked her profusely, then added quietly, 'You don't happen to have any messages for me do you?'

She said, 'Yes.'

My heart was pounding and I felt slightly sick. 'What?' I said.

She said, 'The manager of the Berioska says will you please not go to his shop again?'

Having been promised an evening at the Bolshoi, it came as a great disappointment to learn that we were booked instead at an evening of folklore dancing at the Palace of Congress in the Kremlin. No one seemed to know why. I was all for kicking up a stink, but Mrs Antrobus said, 'In Russia you must let things take their course.'

Had the definite feeling she was trying to tell me something, but what? Could there be more to her than meets the eye? She looks very much the type who might have mixed with the Cambridge crowd in the Thirties.

Suggested walking back with her to hotel after ballet, but she did not rise to any of my baits.

Had barely got back to my room when there was a knock on my door. Opened it to find Belinda Bott who said, after a long pause, 'Well don't you have something to say to me?'

I said, 'I don't think so.'

'Oh,' she said, 'Are you quite sure?' And she pushed her way into the room. Suddenly the whole picture fell into place.

Seizing her by the arm I pushed her into bathroom and turned on all the taps.

'I'm sorry,' she said, 'but I'm not that sort of girl.'

I said, 'Not what sort of girl?'

'Well,' she said, 'you know. . . .'

I said, 'But they did send you, didn't they?'

'Yes, she said.

'And?' I said.

She said, 'And nothing, I just thought, here we are, two people in a strange city without any strings. . . .'

The fact is that, if it weren't for that mirror being where it is, facing the bed, I might easily have been tempted to take her up on her blatant offer. However, one simply cannot afford to risk compromising oneself in a place like Russia. Which reminds me; I still haven't looked at that appliance on the wall.

Monday, November 27th

Up early for a last look at Red Square – on my own. Stood for a while in front of St Basil's looking, in my fur hat, like that famous photograph of Kim Philby, or is it Burgess?

I still couldn't quite believe that I was really there, right under walls of the Kremlin, facing Lenin's marble mausoleum, bang on the very spot where the might of Russia's hardware parades every year before those grim-faced Politburo members.

Was on my way back to the hotel when I realized I was being followed by a young man in a black leather overcoat. The more I quickened my pace the more he hurried after me. Had reached the metro station when I felt a hand on my shoulder. Spun round to be confronted by a grim Slav face beneath a grey fur hat.

'American?' he said in a thick Russian accent. I shook my head.

'British?' I agreed.

He said, 'Would you like to buy a belt? Very nice. Many designs on buckle. Kremlin, Red Star, Head of Lenin. . . .'

'How much?' I said.

'How much you got?' he said.

I got out a Pentel and a couple of sticks of chewing gum.

'Is that all?' he said.

I said, 'How about a couple of bars of Cadbury's Fruit and Nut?'

'Chocolate pah!' he said. 'Don't you have dollars?' I shook my head.

'Forget it,' he said. 'You British all the same. Always trying to get everything on the cheap.'

Hurried back to hotel, looking anxiously about me all the while. Suddenly realized that my new hat was really quite loose. Each time I swivelled my head, the hat stayed where it was. Decided I'd rather have a white patch than a bad fit. Ran up to Berioska to find completely new staff. Also my original hat. Explained problem to new assistant who could not have been nicer and changed it straight away.

Packed suitcase and, out of interest, climbed on chair to examine strange appliance on wall. Managed to unscrew it and was lifting it gently away when leg of chair gave way and I fell back, taking appliance and several wires with me. Left pieces where they were, grabbed suitcase and hurried down to lunch. There seemed to be considerably more activity than usual in the hall – men rushing about with bags of tools, reception clerks busy on the telephone, etc. Mentioned the fact to Irena who said, 'I think there is a problem with the central heating. One of the guests has been interfering with the thermostat in his room.'

To the Tretyakov Gallery for a quick look at the icons before leaving for the airport. Went to collect hat and coat from compulsory cloakroom and was halfway to airport before I realized I had been given someone else's hat by mistake. Not only was it far too large, but it also had an even larger white patch than my own. Oh well. Perhaps it will do as a Christmas present for someone.

Carefully avoided Belinda on plane, but that did not stop her giving me her telephone number. I did not give her mine. Ken and Angela still very much in cahoots right up to the last moment. Surprised however to find her alone on the coach going back to Cromwell Road.

I said, 'Your friend abandoned you then?'

'Yes, thank goodness,' she said. 'At last.'

I was astounded and said that we had all imagined they had really hit it off in a big way.

She said, 'You must be joking. If there's one thing I can't stand it's middle-aged married swingers. I spent most of my free time hiding in my room.'

I said, 'What a shame. I've been wanting to talk to you all weekend.'

'Now he tells me,' she said.

We have exchanged phone numbers. One never knows when one might not find oneself at a loose end in Finchley. Her surname is Tuckerman.

Tuesday, November 28th

Felt curiously detached at the office today. Mentioned to one or two people that I had just spent the weekend in Moscow, but it might just as well have been Margate for all the interest it aroused. Is it any wonder we get on so badly with our Common Market colleagues when we are all so abysmally parochial in our outlook?

Noticed on the way out this evening that someone has at

last been and changed the name on my door. To Stanley Cripps. I give up.

Wednesday, November 29th

To the Rent Tribunal to argue my case against the proposed rise.

The representative of the landlords, a pale runty-looking type with a large moustache that was obviously sapping his strength had little to offer in defence, I thought, and merely re-stated his company's wish to put the rent up. The Rent Officer then announced that, taking everything into consideration, he agreed that the new figure was very much in accord with the rents in that area and that he would be recommending the new rent, to take effect from last September. The two shook hands and it was all over. I left without shaking anyone's hand. A more blatant case of collusion I have yet to encounter. Is it any wonder that intelligent people turn to socialism when this is the way they are treated? Not that some of us have very far to turn.

Thursday, November 30th

The more I think about it, the more I am beginning to harbour grave moral doubts concerning this Teenage Dance I'm supposed to be organizing. In a truly caring society, it's not the haves that need their pockets filled but the have-nots, and I've no doubt Mrs Thatcher is quite capable of keeping her head above water without my help. I am not and never have been anyone's catspaw. It is not too late to withdraw my support for this scheme and I shall write to The Boltons this evening to inform Enid of my decision. I also intend to abandon any ideas I might have had for standing as a Conservative at the next election.

The fact that my change of political heart has occurred shortly after my return from Russia is purely coincidental and anyone who accuses me of starry-eyed opportunism could not be further from the mark. After all, Churchill crossed horses in mid-stream and it certainly did his career no harm in the long run.

December

Friday, December 1st

Rang Bryant-Fenn to say that I should not now be requiring his services on the Teenage Dance Committee. He said, 'That's just as well. I wasn't planning on giving them.'

For all his blatantly capitalist ways, I have always suspected that at heart Hugh is a fellow socialist, and I felt I was quite safe recounting to him my savaging at the hands of the Rent Officer. He was most sympathetic.

He said, 'If I know your landlords, they're selling off every flat that falls vacant, and for a small consideration, they'd be glad to see the back of you.'

I said, 'You've lost me there, comrade.'

'It's quite simple,' he said. 'Write to them – better still ring them up – and say you're thinking of moving, but as things are you can't afford the cost of a van, agent's fees, etc. On the other hand, if they could see their way to covering your expenses to the tune of, say, five thousand smackeroos, you could be on your way tomorrow. They'll jump at it.'

The Labour Party could do with people like Hugh.

Saturday, December 2nd

Hugh rang and said, 'I gather it's all off with Amanda Trubshawe.' No prizes for guessing who he got that bit of tittle-tattle from. I told him that, if he really wanted to know, we'd come to a mutual understanding. 'Yes', he said, 'I thought it was all over. Well you're well out of that one. I speak from experience.' What experience?

Am more than ever convinced that Hugh and she got up to something while I was in America.

Not that it matters a hoot now.

Sunday, December 3rd

Woke feeling lower than a snake's hips.

Mother rang after breakfast today to say that Priscilla had told her she needed a new pair of slippers for Christmas, but if I wanted, she'd get her the slippers and I could think of something else. No news of Tim and Vanessa. I thought they were supposed to be coming back on Thursday?

Ho ho ho.

Nothing worth reading in the papers so spent afternoon picking my eight favourite gramophone records in case I should ever be invited on to 'Desert Island Discs'. It's quite a bit harder than one might imagine.

Monday, December 4th

In the tube this morning an unusually large intake of passengers at Lancaster Gate caught me completely unawares. Put my hand up to prevent myself cannoning into the woman in front of me and suddenly found myself grasping one of her breasts. Unfortunately, there was such a squash I was unable to extricate myself and had to travel all the way to Oxford Circus jammed in this embarrassing position.

The odd thing is that the woman went on reading her *Woman's Realm* apparently without noticing a thing. Perhaps it's something that happens to her every day.

Rang the landlords as soon as I got in and laid my cards on the table more or less along the lines Bryant-Fenn had suggested.

Mr Haynes listened politely, then said, 'We shall certainly be offering your flat for sale when and if you decide to leave. It's no skin off our nose either way, but I would advise you not to try pulling any more tricks of this nature, or you could find yourself in very hot water indeed.'

Obviously the sooner I am out of that place the better. I have rung half a dozen reputable estate agents and they have promised to send me details of houses and flats at the lower end of the price scale.

Tuesday, December 5th

According to the stuff that has arrived from three of the agents, there is nothing for sale below £35,000, and for that one is lucky to get a two-bedroom flat in Tooting.

I see now what the opposition spokesman on the environment meant when he said that those hardest hit by the credit squeeze are the first-time buyers. How on earth does one climb on the property merry-go-round unless one has something to sell? Have I completely missed the boat, I ask myself? Obviously I should have bought something years ago – or better still, I should have abandoned my scruples about living with Amanda.

I've always thought of Parsons Green as being the back of beyond, but I see now that it is every bit as desirable as Belgravia and Mayfair, if not more so.

Wednesday, December 6th

Tim rang after lunch. I was amazed.

'Where are you?' I asked him. 'Russia?'

'Don't be daft,' he said 'I'm in the office. We loved Turkey so much we stayed on a few extra days.'

I felt like asking if they had any cheap houses for sale out there.

'How was Moscow?' he asked.

'It was all right,' I said 'Your friend never got in touch.'

'Who?' he said. 'Belinda?'

I asked him what Belinda had to do with it.

'Nothing, as it turned out,' he said. 'It's just that I suggested she meet up with you. Pity; she's lots of fun. Very much your type I'd have thought.'

I was astonished and said 'Since when have I gone for the Miss Piggy type?'

Tim said, 'Not only is she a lecturer in Russian and an expert on the art treasures of Moscow, but she also happens to be my sister.'

Thursday, December 7th

An astonishing thing happened in the office today.

Returned from an area planning meeting with Pratt to find a message on my desk from Keith Hardacre to say that at long last the New York presentation has borne fruit in the shape of a £250,000 contract. He was with the chairman and would I come up as soon as I got in?

Pratt shook me by the hand and said 'You're made in Barfords now.'

Was in a complete daze as we travelled up in the lift. Arrived in Harold's office to more congratulations and handshakes all round. Harold said, 'I always knew you had it in you,' and opened a bottle of champagne. He then proposed a toast: 'To the young knight who has at last won his spurs.'

As we all trooped out half an hour later, Harold said 'If there's anything I can do to help, don't hesitate to let me know.'

Felt like saying that an interest free loan on a house would not go amiss, but there'll be time for that anon.

In my euphoria, rang Pippa and suggested a celebration dinner at the Bordelino tomorrow night, but maddeningly she's tied up.

Give it time, give it time.

Friday, December 8th

A sensational turn of events. Harold Hill has resigned as Chairman of Barfords and, in the small hours, run away with Pippa to France.

Their precise whereabouts are still a mystery. So far as I am concerned, so is their behaviour. I did not realize that Harold was even aware of Pippa's existence – although the more I think about it, the more everything falls into place.

What can she possibly see in him? Like Mrs Simpson, she cannot seriously believe she is to be the consort of a king in exile.

While I am certainly no killjoy and would deny no one the chance of happiness in this life, I feel personally extremely let down.

After yesterday evening's triumph, I shall obviously be

seen from now on as a Harold Hill man and, with him out of the picture, the knives will soon be out and into my back.

Bang goes my house, if not my career.

Saturday, December 9th

On a whim, rang Angela in Finchley. Hung on for a good two or three minutes but there was no reply which is very odd since she told me she was always at home on Saturdays.

In the evening there was a man on 'Desert Island Discs' I have never heard of in my life. He claimed to be a well-known writer.

Sunday, December 10th

Rang Mollie apropos nothing in particular. She has a theory that all these trades union people are basically failed actors and the only reason they keep going on strike is because it's the only way they can get on TV.

Happened to mention the difficulty I had getting through to Finchley yesterday.

She said, 'What's this girl's name?'

I said Angela Tuckerman.

She screamed with laughter and said, 'Of course nobody answered the phone. On the Sabbath?'

I said sharply that there was no reason to suppose Angela was Jewish.

'With a name like Tuckerman?' she screeched. 'Living in Finchley?'

Monday, December 11th

Instead of going straight home after work, took the bus down to Trafalgar Square for the traditional ceremony of the lighting of the Christmas tree.

It was a most moving occasion and as the Band of the RAF struck up 'The First Nowell', a lump rose in my throat and tears welled up unashamedly in my eyes.

But then isn't that what Christmas is all about?

Tuesday, December 12th

Mother rang with the news I have been dreading all year: Nigel and Priscilla are coming for Christmas, with James. The season of goodwill is obviously destined never to get off the ground this year as far as I am concerned.

Can I honestly be blamed for not being able to raise a lot of enthusiasm about the January sales conference? Hardacre is already showing signs of carping. I'm wondering if I shouldn't have joined the Masons after all. The writing is on the wall.

Angela rang after lunch, much to my delight. Had meant to say nothing about my ringing on Saturday, but it came out anyway.

She said, 'What a shame. The phone was on the blink all day.' Perhaps she is not Jewish after all. Not that it matters a row of beans to me one way or the other. Indeed, I have always understood the Jews to be an unusually warm and generous people. She has suggested an outing tomorrow.

Why I should be so inordinately excited at the prospect of spending an evening with a girl, I don't know, but I am.

Am only sorry that she has seen the Woody Allen film twice.

I said, 'You couldn't face it a third time, I suppose?'

'No' she said.

There's nothing I admire more than a woman who knows her own mind.

Woody Allen's Jewish, of course.

Wednesday, December 13th

I have been out with several women in my life but I do not believe I have felt at once so relaxed and at ease with any of them as I was this evening with Angela. I even quite enjoyed seeing *Players* again.

Dined afterwards at the Bordelino.

It's much farther to Finchley than I thought. I hope this is not going to become a stumbling block.

Thursday, December 14th

To Harley Preston for a meeting about the New York contract.

Ruth Macmichael unnecessarily sharp with me, I thought, Remarked on the fact afterwards to Keith, but all he said was. 'She had a point.'

The knives are very definitely being sharpened. Still, that's big business for you. If you can't stand the heat, get out of the kitchen. That's the way I look at it.

Met Angela for a drink at the Piccadilly Hotel, then back to Holland Park for one of my specials: boeuf bourguignon. She was obviously impressed.

Had a most fascinating talk after dinner about California which she has apparently visited on numerous occasions. She was most interested to hear about my recent visit to New York, although, as she pointed out, there is very little comparison with the West Coast. San Francisco certainly sounds very much my cup of tea, and the news that she is planning to go there next week to live filled me with envy and regret.

I am really going to miss her, and told her so.

She said, 'In that case why not come with me for Christmas and see it for yourself? Who knows, you may like it and decide to stay.'

A tempting offer. However, people in my position do not alter their domestic arrangements at the drop of a hat – not ten days before Christmas, anyway.

Have said I'll think about it.

Friday, December 15th

Today could turn out to be the most momentous of my life.

Was bracing myself for the long haul back to Finchley just before midnight last night when Angela said, 'Do you really want to drive all that way?'

I asked her if she had a better idea.

'Yes,' she said.

I do not propose to go into details about what ensued. I would not wish to embarrass my children and grandchildren when they come to browse through my diary in years to come, and like so many sensitive people, I have always found 'Sportsnight with Coleman' curiously difficult to describe.

Suffice it to say that, if last night was anything to go by, Angela Tuckerman and I were made for each other. Perhaps not on a permanent basis but who knows. . . ?

Whether or not I shall take her up on her offer over America is still something of a moot point. The way things are at Barfords, I shall almost certainly have to start looking for another job soon and America for all its current problems is very much the sort of go-ahead country where I would be able to give free rein to my imagination and talents, as has already been amply proved by my recent success in New York. A £250,000 contract is a £250,000 contract in anyone's language. It is well known that news travels fast in the United States, and I should not be at all surprised to learn that my name is already not entirely unknown in California. Andrew Carnegie, Cary Grant, Dudley Moore – they all seized their chance for fame and fortune in the New World when it came their way, and for me to allow mine to slip through my fingers, for the sake of Christmas with the cat, would be sheer lunacy.

Decisions, decisions. Still, every man must face a watershed at some stage in his life, and only he can decide which is the right path to follow.

Saturday, December 16th

After a largely sleepless night, have finally made up my mind. The crisis is past. America for Christmas it is. I have told Hardacre that I shall be taking a few extra days off over the holiday.

And with these words I lay down my pen and close my diary. Another important chapter of my life draws to a close. Now all I have to do is speak to Mother. She is going to be very cross indeed.